MURDER
SO DEADLY

MURDER
SO DEADLY

A Merry March Mystery

Eileen Curley Hammond

Twody Press

Cover designed by SelfPubBookCovers.com/ RLSather

This book is a work of fiction. Names, characters, places, and incidents
either are products of the author's imagination or are used fictitiously.
Any resemblance to actual persons, living or dead, events, or locales is
entirely coincidental.

Eileen Curley Hammond
Visit my website at www.eileencurleyhammond.com

Printed in the United States of America

First Printing: September 2019
Twody Press

ISBN-978-1-7325460-7-3

Library of Congress Control Number: 2019914509

AUTHOR'S NOTE

Thank you, readers. I hope you are enjoying Merry's journey! And, if you are, please take a moment to pen a review on Amazon and Goodreads. As an independent author, I truly appreciate it!

It's my good fortune to have friends who give their time to help me craft a better story. I'd especially like to thank Jenna Grinstead for her insight, suggestions, and advice. I'd also like to thank Eric Henderson for his eagle eye and consistency. And I'd be remiss if I did not thank April and Shawn VanDervort for sharing their assistance with a plot point. I'd also like to thank the following officers of Buckeye Crime Writers: Connie Berry, Jim Sabin, Patrick Stuart, and Kandy Williams for giving feedback on my first chapter. I appreciate their insight and energy.

Buckeye Crime Writers is always a source of inspiration, education, and support. Their speaker series is great, and through it, I learned about poisons from Dan Baker, Chief Toxicologist for the Franklin County Coroner's office. Thank you, Dan, for sharing your expertise.

I also want to thank Kelly McGuiness for being my touchstone on federal law enforcement.

Any errors in the book are mine, and mine alone.

A big thank you to my editor, Lauren Pan, for keeping me on the straight and narrow, and suggesting good changes; you inspire me.

And finally, thank you to my family. To Caroline Silvey (Artist), who provided a plot idea, Kevin Curley (Playwright), who gives great feedback, and of course, my husband, Robert, who provides encouragement every step of the way.

ALSO BY EILEEN CURLEY HAMMOND

Murder So Sinful
Murder So Festive
Murder So Heartless

For my biggest and most cherished fans in Florida, Aunt Marialyce and Uncle Dick.

CHAPTER 1

Thunder rattled the windows and was followed quickly by a flash of lightning. My two cats cuddled closer, seeming to seek comfort in my warmth. The house groaned as high winds lashed at the exterior walls. I burrowed farther under the covers, eyes wide. Another bolt hit with a boom so loud it seemed to have landed right next door. There was a pause, and then the lights went out.

I yelped and yanked my bedside table drawer open. Fumbling, I found the flashlight. Maybe it was only a circuit breaker. As I made my way downstairs, I stopped by my daughter Jenny's door and eased it open. Soft snores greeted me. I shut the door and scurried down the stairs. Deep shadows in the living room evaded the play of the flashlight. As I ran past, I shivered.

The circuit breakers had been tripped. I said a little prayer and flipped the switches to reset them. Nothing. I turned to go back upstairs. A ghostly white face floated in front of me, and I screamed.

A voice snapped, "Stop that racket. It's bad enough the lights are out."

"Wanda?"

My boyfriend Rob's mother and current houseguest answered, "Who else would it be?"

"What do you have on your face?"

"Cold cream, of course. It moisturizes as I sleep. The storm woke me, so I grabbed the flashlight you left on my dresser. I heard you banging about, so I followed you."

I shuddered. "It's cold."

"Since it's not a breaker, there's no reason for us to dawdle in this dank basement. I'll see you in the morning." The light bobbed as she made her way up the stairs.

I took a deep breath and followed her. My foot hit a damp patch on the concrete floor. *Don't tell me the basement's flooding.* I scanned the perimeter. The rest of the cellar seemed dry. The flashlight lit the stairs, which were marked by damp footprints. Why were her feet wet? I was focused on her face, so I never looked to see what she was wearing. The wind continued to howl.

✳ ✳ ✳

The next morning came far too early. I was huddled over my coffee when a creak from the third stair made the hairs on my arms salute. *I can't believe she's only been here for two days. It feels like two years.* I leaped up and grabbed another coffee mug. Wanda strutted into the kitchen. The light floral aroma of Jean Patou's Joy scented the air. Her hair was teased and shellacked into a careful bob, and her makeup, though heavy, was expertly applied.

I poured cream into the coffee and handed it to her. "Here you go, just the way you like it. That was some storm."

"It was." She took a sip and pursed her lips. "It's not hot enough." She pushed it away.

I gritted my teeth and placed the mug in the microwave. "This should do the trick."

Her well-manicured left eyebrow rose. "Microwaved coffee. What a treat." She sat at the counter, smoothed her Lilly Pulitzer flowered dress, and examined her French manicure. "I've been thinking. You really should do something about your hair."

I patted my shoulder-length curls. "What's wrong with my hair?"

"That color. It's red."

"It's my natural color. I like it."

2

"There's nothing wrong with helping nature. That's what stylists are for. Maybe when you and Rob come to visit, I'll have my guy try to do something with you." She gave me an appraising glance. "And maybe your makeup. Perhaps a different color liner."

I bit my tongue. I'll visit you when hell freezes over.

"At any rate, I need to go out today. You don't need your car, do you?"

I stifled a groan. "I had planned on going to the other side of town to check on one of the claims, but I guess I could walk or go tomorrow."

"Good. I'll be back in time for dinner. What are you making?"

"Lasagna?"

She stood. "Too heavy with all that cheese and carbs. You need to be setting a better example for your daughter. Pick up salmon and a nice salad; it's much healthier." She took my keys and waltzed out, the door slamming behind her.

Jenny's head poked around the corner. "Is she gone?"

"Barely."

"Good." Jenny hurried into the kitchen, filled a glass full of orange juice, and downed it in three gulps. "I still don't understand why she's staying with us and not Mr. Jenson."

"We've been through this before. We're helping Rob out. Wanda and her husband fought, and her husband is staying at Rob's until they go home or make up. Thank goodness they're only here for another week."

"Mom, this is like her fifth husband. I don't know anyone who's been married so many times. If they're not getting along, does that mean there'll be a sixth?" Jenny's bright blue eyes widened. "Can people be married that often?"

"I'm sure they'll patch things up."

Jenny selected an apple from the fruit bowl. "You're such an optimist. See you later." Her blonde ponytail swung behind her as she bounded out the door.

I tossed Wanda's untouched coffee into the sink and put the mug in the dishwasher. *I'm going to kill that woman.*

I picked up my briefcase and stormed out. A seventy-plus woman with long gray hair waved to me from the back stoop of the house next door. "Howdy, neighbor! Some storm last night!"

Taking a deep breath, I straightened my shoulders and strode to where she was standing. I held out my hand. "It was. We met the other week when you moved in, but with all the movers coming and going, I don't know if you remember me, Meredith March. My friends call me Merry."

"Of course I remember you. Alex Danford." She smiled and shook my hand. "It was crazy that day. It's good to meet you officially." She wore a shapeless dress that hung to mid-calf, and her feet looked comfortably ensconced in Birkenstocks.

"I'm sorry that I haven't been able to get to know you better, it's been busy at work, and now I have a guest staying with me. I'll bring some freshly baked muffins tomorrow to make it up to you."

"That sounds great. A word of warning, no nuts, please. I'm allergic. Just bang on the back door. It's always open. I haven't met that many people in town yet. Andy and Ed—" she pointed to the house beyond the alley—"came over the other day. They're going to give me a party to rectify that."

"We'll be there. Ed's some cook. You'll enjoy it." I pointed to a new, ornate, structure in the far left corner of her backyard. It looked Victorian, black with steeples and clear window insets. "Is that a greenhouse? I saw the men assembling it last week."

She nodded. "It's small, but it gets the job done. I like to putter in the garden. Whoever lived here before had a green thumb. I love all the plants."

"The woman who previously owned the house was a good friend and a great gardener."

"Her cousin told me what happened. It's hard to believe your friend was murdered in such a lovely spot." Alex whispered, "She said it happened in the kitchen."

"It did." I shuddered. "It was sad, but at least they caught the person responsible. It's safe now."

Alex motioned toward my briefcase. "I can see you're on your way to work, so I won't keep you. If you ever want a tour of the greenhouse, let me know. I've taken several people through."

"I'll take you up on that. See you tomorrow morning."

I ambled toward downtown Hopeful. Some small tree limbs and shingles littered the yards of a few people, but those were the only remnants of the storm from the previous night. The daffodils were on their last gasp, and the hyacinths were almost fully open. Their sweet scent was almost overpowering. A warm southerly breeze caressed the hanging baskets of tulips lining Main Street. I made my way along the brick storefronts, turning in at the property and casualty insurance agency I owned, the Meredith March Insurance Agency. My assistant, Cheryl, greeted me with a warm smile. Her long blonde hair was swept into a professional bun. "Rob's on the phone. He said he called your cell, but he wasn't able to get through."

I pulled my phone from my purse and sighed. "I forgot to charge it last night. Not that it would have done much good with the power being out."

Cheryl took it from me. "I have your extra charger at my desk. How's Rob's mother?"

"Not leaving soon enough." I clasped my hand over my mouth. "I can't believe I said that. Chalk it up to stress." I walked into my office and pressed speaker. "Hi, Rob, what's up?"

"I miss you. And, Richard is driving me up a wall. If he smokes one more cigar inside, I'm going to throttle him. Did you lose power?"

"For a little while. Something strange happened when I was checking the fuses—your mother came down to the basement to see what was happening, and when she left, the floor was damp. I didn't hear the shower. How did she get wet?"

"Did you ask her about it?"

My jaw clenched. "No. I was distracted by her critique of the color of my hair and how I make coffee." I sighed. "Scratch that. Your mother is a delightful guest." I bit the inside of my cheek.

He laughed. "I love my mother, but she can be demanding."

"Uh-huh." I popped an antacid in my mouth.

"You're such a nice person, Merry March. I owe you one." He paused. "This is nuts. They came to visit me, and now they're inconveniencing you. Why don't we all go out to dinner tonight and see if we can get them talking? I'll give Mother a call and then let Richard know. I'll text you the arrangements."

"Your mother will go crazy if the place doesn't list calories on the menu. She wanted to know the count of everything I've made."

"I know the perfect spot. Love you."

"Love you too." I hung up and did a few shoulder exercises to try and loosen my neck muscles. Rob Jenson was worth the temporary pain and suffering his mother was inflicting on me. And, if I were lucky, my annulment would come through, and I could marry him. But then Wanda would be my mother-in-law. I gulped, and my neck tensed all over again.

Cheryl walked in with the day's call list and pointed to the fifth name. "You may want to move this woman to the top of the list. She closed on her house, and she's worried she won't be covered."

"Okay. I'll start with her. Anything else pressing?"

"Quite a few people called with roof damage after that storm last night, but the staff has been handling those."

I doodled on my note pad. "It sounded like a freight train at times. Not to mention the thunder and lightning. I saw some limbs down on my way here. While it's fresh in everyone's minds, why don't you send out a note advising people to clear out dead trees and branches from around their houses?" I picked up the phone and began my calls.

* * *

I hurried home to change. In short-order, Jenny, Wanda, and I were in the car and on our way to the restaurant. I turned on the radio to mask the strained silence. When we pulled into the parking lot, Rob and his stepfather, Richard Franco, were walking into Fiorella's. Rob's blond hair gleamed in the waning sunlight, and his mustache twitched as if Richard had told a joke. Richard waddled, his girth seeming to slow him. Richard was shorter than Rob and a few decades older. They waited for us in the lobby, which was brightly lit with warm wood tones.

Richard leaned in for a kiss, but Wanda didn't miss a beat. She walked right past him and followed the hostess to our table. My mouth dropped, and Rob's eyebrow rose. Richard gave his phone a quick glance, but his shoulders sagged as he turned to follow. Rob went next, and Jenny and I brought up the rear. The hostess brought us to a round table covered by a white tablecloth, which had a small vase of sweet pea and roses as its centerpiece. I gave Jenny's hand a quick squeeze. Rob motioned for her to sit on one side of him and his mother the other. Richard took the seat next to Wanda, and I sat between him and Jenny.

Richard said, "It's good to see you, Wanda. It's been hard to be here without you."

Wanda leaned around Rob. "Jenny, why don't you switch places with me?"

Jenny grabbed my hand, but before I could intervene, Rob moved his chair closer to the table, effectively blocking his mother's line of sight. "We're adults; we should be able to have one civil meal together."

Wanda sniffed, "If you say so." She picked up the menu. "Good. They have fish. And look, they list the calories. All places should do that."

"You look lovely as usual. All that discipline has paid off. I wish I could show some." Richard patted his stomach.

"It wouldn't kill you to work out more." Her eyebrow arched. "Or eat less."

Rob put down his menu. "Everyone can order what they want, and no one is going to criticize anyone else's choices." He turned to me. "Merry, anything interesting happen today?"

"We had a few claims as a result of that storm last night."

"We were lucky it wasn't as bad in town as it was east. I took a picture of a barn that had a tree sticking out of it. With the number of dead ash trees we have around here, we're lucky more didn't topple." Rob unfolded his napkin onto his lap.

The waitress came to take our orders. Wanda spoke first, "Salmon plain, lightly grilled. No sauce, no butter. And a side of spinach, again, no butter."

"Got it."

I really wanted the lasagna, but Wanda was staring right at me as I ordered. I kicked myself as I said, "Scallops please, with the broccoli."

Wanda piped up, "Surely, you want that cooked without butter."

I sighed. "No butter."

Jenny went next. "I'll have the lasagna please."

Wanda coughed.

"I play basketball and dance. I need the calories."

Rob smiled. "Yes, you do. How about splitting some garlic bread with me?"

Jenny sat back in her chair. "Love to."

Richard ordered the stuffed shells.

Dinner arrived, and I picked at my scallops. They would have tasted much better drenched in butter. Jenny's lasagna looked fantastic. All bubbly and cheesy, the way I liked it. The garlic bread arrived and enveloped the table with a lovely aroma. Rob passed the basket, and I showed enormous willpower by only taking one slice.

Wanda stared. I bit into the bread and gave her a broad smile. "You should have some. It's wonderful."

The rest of the evening was equally tense. As we left the restaurant, I gave Rob a kiss goodnight, then whispered, "Maybe we should trade houseguests."

He kissed me back. "Trust me, Richard's no prize."

Richard and Wanda stood to the side, speaking softly to each other.

Jenny climbed into the back, and Wanda took the passenger seat, a small smile on her face. "The salmon was good."

* * *

I rose early to bake muffins for Alex. After they cooled, I put them in a cloth-lined basket. Then I ran into my office, pulled out a piece of notepaper, and scribbled "Welcome to the neighborhood. Hope you enjoy the muffins, Merry." The clock chimed seven. I hoped that it wasn't too early. I scooted out the back door and up the steps to my new neighbor's house, hesitating before knocking. The last time I'd been at this door was when my ex-husband rented it earlier in the year. He left town right before the FBI stormed in to arrest him. I patted my pockets for an antacid. Empty. I straightened my shoulders, wreathed my face in a smile, and knocked softly, in case Alex was still asleep. The door opened. She was fully dressed and wearing a beige smock smeared with a kaleidoscope of colors.

I handed her the muffins.

"I wasn't sure what type you liked, so I went with my favorite, Morning Glory. And don't worry. No nuts."

She waved me into the house and lifted the basket closer to her face. "They smell wonderful."

"Do you paint?"

"Landscapes and flowers mostly. The early morning light is wonderful."

"I'd love to see your work sometime."

"Won't you join me for coffee?"

"I'm sorry, I really can't stay; I have a busy morning. Are you free for lunch on Saturday? I'd love to get to know you better."

"Sounds lovely. Noon?"

"That works." I hurried down the stairs, across the driveway, and up the steps back into my kitchen. I reached for my car keys, but they weren't on the counter next to the garage, where I usually dropped them. I groaned and scurried upstairs. Knocking softly on the guest room door, I whispered, "Wanda, are you awake?"

There was no response. I inched the door open. The bed was made, and Wanda was not in the room. I looked down the hallway. The bathroom door was open; no one was in there. I ran back down the stairs, checked my office, and the laundry room. *Where is she?*

I stuck my head in the garage. No car. When had she gone out? I went to bed before her, but I hadn't heard her leave. I ran back up the stairs. The bathroom door was now closed. I knocked, and Jenny opened the door, curling iron in hand. "I thought you left for work."

"Have you seen our houseguest?"

"She isn't in her room?"

"Nope."

"Weird." She turned her attention back to the mirror.

I texted Rob: "Do you know where your mother is?"

My phone rang. "She's not with you?"

"Her bed hadn't been slept in, and the car's MIA."

There was a pause and then a quick knock. "Richard?" A door creaked. "Richard's not here either."

"Where do you think they are?"

Rob sighed. "They're adults. Let's not worry about it. They'll return eventually."

"Easy for you to say. Your mom has my car."

"Want mine?"

I scrolled my calendar. "If it wouldn't be a problem."

"I'll drop it by in ten minutes."

I hung up and poured myself another cup of coffee. The cats eyed me and mewed, so I tossed them a few treats. "I'll let you out later."

Jenny ran by, picking up a banana on her way out.

"Have more than—" I was talking to the door.

There was a quick knock, and Rob strolled in. "Where do you think they are?"

"Together, I hope. Especially since Wanda has my car." I held out my hand for Rob's keys. "Want me to drop you somewhere?"

"My office?"

"No problem."

✳ ✳ ✳

I was kissing him goodbye when his phone rang. He answered, "Mom, where are you? You have Merry's car—" his eyes widened, and his jaw dropped. "Room 212? I'll be right there."

He hung up and turned to me. "Richard's dead. They're at the motel near the highway. I'll need the car."

"I'm coming with you." I pulled back onto the road and made a left at the traffic light. "He's so overweight. Was it his heart?"

"She didn't know. She woke up, and he was dead."

We arrived at the "no-tell" motel. We ran up the concrete stairs to the second floor and turned right. Midway down the corridor, a room was cordoned off by yellow police tape. Rob said, "They got here quickly."

A pallid young man wearing a brown motel uniform, stood just outside the tape, cell phone in his hands. "This has never happened before. I called the manager, and she's on her way."

I asked, "Do you know what happened?"

He shook his head. "No. The lady in the room called down and said her husband was dead. I called the police. They just got here."

Detective Jay Ziebold, our friend and sometime collaborator on murder cases, walked out of the room. His hand gripped Wanda's arm. I gasped. Her hair was askew, mascara streaked her face, and the dress she wore from the night before was beyond wrinkled. She looked ready for a perp walk.

The young man pointed his phone at her. I held my hand in front of it. "No recording."

He huffed and put the phone down.

Rob moved so that he blocked Jay. "Where are you taking her?"

Jay stopped. "What's your involvement in this?"

"She's my mother."

Jay groaned. "I should have guessed once I heard her name. Why are you two involved in all my cases?" He rubbed his forehead. "The medical examiner is working on the body, so I'm taking Ms. Jenson to the station for questioning."

"I'll join you."

Wanda stood straighter. "Call my attorney. He'll know someone good in the area."

Rob blanched. "Why would you need a lawyer? Richard died of natural causes."

Jay replied, "We're not sure what happened yet. Come along, Ms. Jenson. Your attorney can meet us at the station."

"Surely I can go back to Merry's and clean up first."

"I'm sorry, but no. Let's get this out of the way."

It looked like Wanda was going to argue with him, but then her shoulders slumped, and she allowed herself to be led down the stairs.

A moment later, the medical examiner wheeled out Richard's sheet-covered body. I said a quick prayer. Rob edged closer. "Mind if I take a look?"

The medical examiner glared and brushed past him to the elevator. "Reporters!"

Rob pulled out his phone. He pressed in a number, turned, and talked quietly into it.

I stood in the corridor, outside the room's open door. Two techs appeared to be gathering evidence. They were in the process of bagging a bottle of champagne that lay on the floor. The sheets were rumpled. Rob joined me. "Looks like it was a busy night."

"Unfortunately it had a horrible ending."

CHAPTER 2

I used my spare keys to retrieve the car, then drove to check on clients who had suffered the worst damage from the storm. It was sad to see all the shingles strewn across the grass like cards. Having dispensed referrals for roof repairs, I returned to my office. I hung up my coat, and Cheryl walked in. "Did you hear what happened at the motel? I heard someone died."

I sank onto my chair. "It was Rob's stepfather."

She sat opposite me. "You're kidding."

"I wish I were." I put my purse in a drawer. "Do me a favor. Doesn't your sister-in-law work at the police station now?"

"Yes."

"Would you ask her to let you know when Wanda leaves?"

"Wanda's at the station? Did she kill her husband?"

"I don't think so. At this point, I'm not sure what happened."

"Good thing it was him. If it were her, you'd be a prime suspect."

"Not funny." I pointed toward the door.

I texted Rob: "Anything?"

"Attorney arrived. Waiting at the station."

"Keep me posted."

I put down my cell and started on my call list. I made my way through most of it, and as I was about to leave for lunch, Cheryl breezed in. "Your future mother-in-law has been set free."

"Thanks." I picked up my cell and typed, "Lunch at my house?"

Rob replied: "Going there now."

I gathered what I needed to work on the rest of the day and waved to Cheryl on my way out.

When I pulled in the driveway, Rob was outside waiting for me. "She's in the shower."

"That's not surprising; she had a tough night." I gave him a quick kiss and walked into the kitchen. I washed my hands and started pulling things out for a salad. "What did she say?"

"Not a lot. She seemed confused."

"When did they cook up the scheme to meet at the motel?"

"Must have been right before we got in the car."

"Oh. So that's what they were whispering about."

Wanda walked into the kitchen. She wore no makeup, her hair had not been dried, and she looked about ten years older. She stared at the salad spinner in my hand. "No. That won't do. I need something more." She turned to Rob. "Do you still make those grilled cheesed sandwiches?"

My mouth dropped. Who is this woman?

Rob kissed his mother on the forehead. "For you, anything."

She sank to a chair at the kitchen table, and I joined her. "What happened?"

"Tea?"

Rob said, "I'll get it." He put the kettle on.

I stared into her brown eyes.

She shifted in her chair. "We made up. I forgave him for not giving me the birthday present I wanted."

I waited.

"I wanted to go on a cruise through the Panama Canal." She inspected her nails. "We won't be going now."

I barely restrained myself from a major eye roll. "I'm sorry you won't be able to go on your cruise now that your husband died. What happened last night?"

"We decided to meet at the Shady Inn." She sniffed. "That's not the kind of hotel I had in mind. I normally stay at the Ritz Carlton."

"Sorry, we don't have one in town."

She looked up at me. "Was that sarcasm?"

"I wish we did have a nice hotel in town." I bit my lip.

"Anyway, I stopped at the wine shop you showed me, Pick of the Vine—tawdry little place—to pick up a bottle of French champagne. I had to get a bottle of prosecco, if you can imagine. I mean, doesn't anyone celebrate in this town?"

I moved my index finger in a clock motion, signaling for her to speed up. "You were saying—"

"Richard called me with the room number, and I went directly there." She rubbed her arm. "He popped the prosecco, and we drank it out of those horrid small plastic cups." Her gaze lingered on my cupboard. "I wish I had thought to take some glasses."

Rob placed a beautifully toasted sandwich with cheese just beginning to ooze and a cup of tea in front of his mother. She lifted a corner and said, "Good, you didn't burn it. You always used to put the burnt side down to hide it."

He handed me my sandwich. I smiled up at him. "Perfect, like you."

He rubbed my shoulder and sat at the table. "Continue, Mother."

"We had some champagne and did some celebrating. Around two in the morning, Richard started to feel ill and woke me. I assured him it was the cheap wine and went back to sleep. In the morning he was lying on the bathroom floor, dead. I can't believe I've lost another husband."

I asked, "Do you need help making arrangements? Do you know where he'd like to be buried?"

Her bright brown eyes darkened. "May as well be here. You might actually be helpful. He didn't have many friends, so you might be able to get people you know to come to the funeral. I'd hate to have no one come." She sipped her tea. "That is once they release his body."

Rob put potato chips on his plate. "He was pretty old. I'm sure that they'll figure out it was natural causes."

His mother glared at him. "He was the same age as me, seventy-two. That's not old." She paused. "I wish your sister was here. She always treats me so well."

I bit my tongue, gathered the dirty dishes, and Rob helped load them into the dishwasher. His mother rose and strolled from the room. "I'm going to put my face on, if anyone cares."

I leaned against Rob's shoulder. "Wow."

He wiped the counter. "That about sums it up. I'm sorry I saddled you with her."

"It hasn't been that bad."

"Uh-huh. After we get mother through the next few weeks, we'll have to do something fun. Just the two of us."

I hugged him. "That sounds wonderful."

✳ ✳ ✳

"Let me get this straight. You're helping your potential future mother-in-law plan the funeral for her yet to be released fifth husband's body. Has anyone ever told you your life is complicated?" My best friend, Patty Twilliger, sipped her wine.

"Yep."

She removed a white scrunchie and fluffed her long brown hair. "I do love you, but you are showing latent doormat tendencies. I don't understand it. You're so strong at work, yet at home, you let everyone walk all over you. And what are you doing here?" She swept her arm to encompass her comfortable living room. She had chosen a cottage décor that would stand up well to kids, yet look elegant enough for adults.

I sank farther into her soft, blue sofa. "I'm hiding. Be nice. I'm tired of being berated." I swirled my wine. " And besides, what am I supposed to do? He's dead, and she doesn't know anyone in town. I have to help."

"Doesn't he have any other relatives?"

"He has a daughter, but they haven't spoken in years."

"Is she coming to the funeral?"

"I don't know. Wanda said she was considering inviting her. Rob's sister, Elizabeth Jenson, is coming into town tomorrow. Rob and I may have both our houses full."

"Can't Elizabeth and Wanda stay at Rob's?"

I took a long sip of wine and contemplated my glass. "They could, but Wanda said that being at Rob's would be too painful because it would remind her of Richard. Not that she's shed a single tear since he died."

"She sounds like a marvelous person."

Jenny, and Patty's daughter Cindy, came rushing down the stairs. Jenny plopped down next to me. "Mom, can I stay here tonight?" She batted her long eyelashes at me.

"You're going to make me go back there all alone?"

"Please."

"Okay, but that means you'll have to get up early to come home and dress for school."

Cindy offered, "She can borrow something from me."

I kissed Jenny's cheek. "Rat."

She stood. "Thanks, Mom." They ran back upstairs.

I took my wine glass into the kitchen. "It's late. I should be getting back."

I shivered as I stepped into the cool night air. Pulling my coat tighter, I scurried back to the house. I opened the door, dropped my purse on the kitchen stool, and shrugged out of my jacket. Wanda sat at the kitchen table, drinking a glass of wine. "It's about time you got home. You should have more sympathy for me." She took a large gulp. "I just lost my husband."

I sat down. "I made progress on the arrangements this morning."

"You did?"

"Yes, I spoke with Father Tom, and he's agreed to hold the funeral mass."

"Oh, do we have to go through all that falderal? Can't he say a few words and be done with it?"

I shook my finger at her. "You put me in charge; we're going to have a full mass. No shortcuts."

"Very well." She sighed. "I hope you've been thinking about food."

"I have. The people who live behind us, Andy Perkins and his husband Ed, own an antiques store and tea shop in town. I'm going to ask them to cater lunch for us here."

Her eyes narrowed. "You're going to hire out the catering? That sounds expensive. I thought you were supposed to be a good cook."

"Not as good as Ed. I want to be able to thank everyone who comes, and I won't be able to do that if I have to worry about replenishing the food."

"I'm not paying for that."

I bit the inside of my cheek and struggled to remain calm. "When is Elizabeth getting here?"

"Her plane gets in tomorrow at ten. I told her you'd pick her up at the airport."

I stood, retrieved a wine glass, and poured myself a large portion. After a long sip, I put the glass down. "I'd be happy to. Have her text me the plane info."

"Can't you get it from her? I hate being the go-between. Rob has her number."

My grip on the wine glass grew tight. Courvoisier, one of my cats, rubbed against my leg. I sank my fingers into her fur and petted her. My hand relaxed. I stood. "We'll work out the details. I'll see you in the morning." I took my wine glass, topped it off, and moved carefully up the stairs so that I wouldn't spill a single drop.

I sat on the bed, took a long drink, and picked up my phone.

"Send me your sister's phone number."

Rob replied with the number.

"Thanks."

"Love you." He appended an emoji hug.

I sent him a heart emoji and put my phone down. I propped myself up on the pillows and reached for my book. Courvoisier and my other cat, Drambuie, soon joined me. One settled by my legs, and the other climbed on my chest. I took another sip of wine and leaned down to whisper in Courvoisier's ear, "She'll be leaving soon, won't she?"

* * *

The next day brought a flurry of activity. Rob decided to pick up his sister, so that left me free to finalize the details of the funeral with Father Tom and then, later, Ed. I sat at the kitchen counter and pulled the phone toward me. First on my list was Jay. "Jay, do you know when the coroner will release Richard's body?"

"When I spoke to her yesterday, she thought she'd be able to do the autopsy by Thursday. That means they'll probably release him on Friday."

"So it would be safe to schedule the funeral for Monday?"

"That should be okay."

I hung up and scratched "check with Jay" from my list. Feeling accomplished, I poured myself another cup of coffee. My phone buzzed with a text from Jenny: "I know you have lots going on, but okay if I stay at Cindy's tonight?"

"You have to come home eventually."

"I'll pick up clothes at three."

The phone rang. Seeing that it was Cheryl, I answered. "What's up?"

"We're having some problems with one of the storm claims. If I send you the information, would you give the insurance company a call?"

"No problem. I'll be on the lookout." I hung up.

There was a quick rap at the back door, and Ed strolled in. He held out a dish. "I was thinking lemon squares for the reception after the funeral. Let me know what you think."

The square was a deep yellow and was dusted with powdered sugar. I pulled a fork from the drawer and used the side of it to cut myself a bite. "I love the crust. It's so light and buttery. And the lemon is so tart. Is that a piece of candied lemon on the top?"

He nodded.

"This is a winner." I pushed the plate toward him.

He slid the plate back in my direction. "You can have the rest. I'll bring some other things by for you to try tomorrow."

"Thanks. I heard from Jay. We'll have the funeral on Monday."

"That works out well. Monday's normally a slow day. See you later." The door shut behind him.

I eyed the rest of the lemon bar. Giving in, I pulled it toward me, took another small bite, and smacked my lips. *So good.*

"What are you eating?"

I jumped. Wanda walked to the counter and eyed the remains of the lemon bar.

"It's one of the desserts Ed is going to make for the funeral."

"Is that the size he's serving? It doesn't seem very large."

"I ate half of it."

Wanda's eyebrow arched.

There was another knock at the door, and Rob came in. "Mother, I thought you might want to join me for the ride to the airport."

I flashed him a grateful smile.

"Sure. It will be good to see Elizabeth. Let me get my coat." She walked up the stairs.

I groaned. "I hate to say anything, but your mother is a teeny bit judgmental."

He tapped my nose with his finger. "More than a teeny bit. May I?" He pointed toward the dessert.

"Have at it."

He took a bite. "This is good. How much butter is in this?"

I shook my head. "I don't want to know."

"Are you sure you don't want more?"

"Yep. I've lost my appetite."

"Hopefully you'll be hungry by this evening. I thought we'd go to the Golden Skillet."

"Jenny's staying at Cindy's tonight, and I'm tired. Would you mind if I begged off? I'm sure you'd like some alone time with your mom and sister."

Rob walked around the counter and hugged me from behind. "I'm sensing a cry for help."

I leaned back into his arms. "You may be right."

"Okay. I'll take the two of them to dinner and drop Mother off at bedtime."

Wanda cleared her throat. Rob gave me one last squeeze and kissed the top of my head. "See you later."

I washed Ed's plate, dried it, and left it on the counter so I would remember to bring it back. Then I strolled to the office to try and get something done for a few hours. It was busy and, by the end of the day, it felt like the phone was permanently glued to my ear.

I locked up and started to amble back to my house. I hadn't gone more than four steps when someone said, "Wait up. I'll walk with you." I turned. Andy hurried to catch up, his long legs making it look easy. "What are you doing tonight?"

"Nothing." I smiled. "Absolutely nothing. I have the evening free. I might even take a long bath."

"Ed's making a new shepherd's pie recipe if you want to have dinner with us."

I stopped, considering. "Would it be rude if I came to eat and left right after dinner?"

He put his arm around my shoulders and squeezed. "You and Jenny are like family. Leave whenever you want, as long as you bring wine." He winked.

"I'll be there." I unlocked the back door and walked into the house. The cats danced around my feet, waiting to be fed. That task accomplished, I gave my hair a quick brush, took a bottle of Merlot out of the wine fridge, picked up Ed's plate, and waltzed out the door.

Andy held the door open for me as I ran up their back steps. I handed him the wine.

"Thanks," he said.

I took off my coat and put it in the closet. The house smelled wonderful, like roasted garlic, onions, and carrots. I gave Ed a quick kiss on the cheek, walked around the counter, and sat. My stomach growled. "Andy said it was a new recipe?"

"It is. I roasted the vegetables then put the short ribs with some wine and onions in the slow cooker this morning. Some mashed potatoes and all I had to do was shred the meat, fold in the veggies, and pop it in the oven. "

Andy handed me a glass of wine. I toasted Ed, "To the organized chef."

He smiled. "To guinea pigs."

Andy sat down next to me. "What do you think of the new neighbor? She's quite the painter."

"She seems nice. We were supposed to have lunch this Saturday, but, with everything that's going on, I had to cancel."

"Don't forget our party the Saturday after next. It'll be crowded, but maybe you'll get a chance to speak with her then."

"Hopefully, our houseguest will have left by then."

Andy nudged my shoulder. "So what happened with Rob's stepfather? I heard that his mother was caught at the "no-tell" motel with him."

I rubbed the back of my neck. "He died, and yes, they were at the Shady Inn. I'm not sure what happened."

Ed grabbed potholders, took the casserole dish from the oven, and placed it on the trivet. His grey eyes lifted to mine. "Do you think she killed him?"

"Don't be silly. I'm sure they'll find that he died of natural causes." I traced the veining of the island countertop. "I hope."

CHAPTER 3

After dawdling in bed reading and finally venturing forth for a quick bout of stretching, I felt ready to face the day. I texted Jenny: "You up?"

"I am now."

"Dinner tonight; be here by six to meet Rob's sister."

"If I must."

"Love you."

I received a heart in return.

I snuck down the stairs hoping that I'd be able to slink out the door before Wanda woke up. Unfortunately, she was sitting by the door, already dressed for the day. She smirked, "A bit late, isn't it?"

"It is. So I need to leave. Now."

She waved her hand, dismissing the urgency in my voice. "I have a favor to ask. Richard's daughter decided to come to the funeral. She'll be arriving on Saturday. She could have Jenny's room, and Jenny could sleep on the couch."

I squelched a groan. "Can't she stay at Rob's?"

"She'd be on the couch there. Here she'd have a bed. I don't know her that well, but it seems more welcoming."

"But then Jenny would be on the couch."

"She's been at her friend's the last few nights. What difference does it make?"

"Let me talk to Jenny about it. I'll let you know tonight." I sighed.

"Can you leave your keys? I may want to go out later."

I dropped them on the counter and slid past her out the door. Clenching my purse, I ran down the back stairs and race-walked toward the driveway. My new neighbor, Alex, had her easel set up outside in the backyard. I forced a smile and waved. "You're taking advantage of the nice weather."

"I am. It's lovely this morning."

I took a deep breath, checked my watch, and walked toward her. I looked over her shoulder. She had painted a grouping of daffodils. Some were the standard yellow, some were rimmed with yellow, and others had a yellow center surrounded by creamy white flowers. "That's beautiful. You've captured the moment."

She pointed with her paintbrush. "It's this yard. It gives me such inspiration. I love flowers. Especially exotic ones. Though these are nice too."

"I'll let you get back to it."

I texted Rob as I walked to work. "Pick me up at four for food shopping? Dinner tonight at my house."

"Sounds good. See you then."

I had an appointment with the accountant to finalize my taxes, so the day was a blur of forms, deductions, and income. I was surprised when I saw Rob in my doorway. "You're early." He pointed behind me. I turned and checked the clock. "I stand corrected; you are right on time, as usual." I stood and stretched. "My accountant left. I think I've got my taxes nailed down."

He kissed me. "Sounds like you deserve a drink."

"I do. But let's get to the grocery store and figure out what's for dinner first."

He drove me to the store. "What are you in the mood for?"

"Let's see what looks good. Is your sister as particular as your mother?"

He laughed. "No. She's normal, like me. You're going to love her."

Rob pushed the shopping cart while I surveyed the fish. "The salmon looks good, and I know your mother will eat that."

"My sister likes it too."

"Sold." I told the clerk how much I wanted. "Let's go to the salad bar and load up on several different options to make it easy for people to pick what they like."

We stood in the slow-moving checkout line. Finally, it was our turn. The chatty cashier started scanning our items. "Did you hear about the guy who was killed at the motel by his wife?"

Rob's mouth dropped. "They don't know what happened yet. I'm sure it was natural causes."

I inserted my credit card to pay.

The clerk leaned over the conveyor belt and lowered her voice. "That's not what I heard. And I hear plenty in this job."

Rob seemed rooted to the floor.

I took his hand. "Let's go. It's getting late."

He glared at the clerk, and we left. "I can't believe that woman. That's my mother she's gossiping about." He shoved the bags into the trunk.

I touched his arm. "Treat the bags nicer. We want to eat tonight."

"I'm sorry. This is all so strange." We got in the car, and Rob drove me home.

We each grabbed a few bags from the trunk and were able to make it into the kitchen in one trip. Wanda and Elizabeth sat on the window seat, drinking tea.

Elizabeth wore a rainbow-colored striped sweater, brown slacks, and penny loafers. She was tall, thin, and had blonde hair pulled into a haphazard bun.

I held out my hand. She disregarded it and wrapped me in a big hug. "I've heard so much about you."

My face heated up. "All good things I hope."

Rob said, "Of course."

"And you own your own business. I like enterprising women." She finally let me go. I took a step back.

Wanda interjected, "You know Elizabeth is a doctor. A surgeon."

"Yes, Rob told me. That's impressive."

She waved her hand. "It pays the bills. Plus I love helping people." She peeked in one of the shopping bags. "What are we having for dinner? I'm starving."

I showed her the assortment of things we bought. "Let me get some hors d'oeuvres going."

"I'll help." She walked around the counter into the kitchen.

I pulled out a few kinds of cheese, carrots, and celery. "If you could get started on those, I can pull together a quick crumble for dessert."

She washed and peeled the carrots, then cut them into precise, smaller sticks. I took the pitted cherries from the freezer and tossed them with flour, cinnamon, a little salt, and a touch of vanilla. Then I put flour, oats, and a stick of butter into the stand mixer. Wanda joined us. "You aren't going to use all that butter, are you?"

I lifted my eyes to hers. "I have some fresh yogurt and berries in the refrigerator if you would rather have that."

She harrumphed.

Elizabeth said, "I'm having the crumble. It sounds delicious."

I placed the dessert into the oven and set the timer.

Rob uncorked a bottle of wine. "Who wants some?" Elizabeth and I nodded.

Wanda lifted her glass. "I already have some."

Jenny eased through the back door as if she hoped she was invisible. I hugged her. "I've missed you."

She squirmed free. I introduced her to Elizabeth.

Elizabeth shook her hand. "Rob said you're a great basketball player. I used to play when I was your age. I'm in a volleyball league now."

I picked up my wine and the nibbles. "Let's go into the living room. It's more comfortable."

Jenny sat on the hearth, Wanda sat on one of the armchairs, and Rob and his sister sat on the couch. I hesitated for a moment and then sat in the other chair. I put the munchies down. "How was your trip, Elizabeth?"

"Not too bad. The planes were on time for once. I liked that restaurant last night—" She looked at Rob.

"Golden Skillet."

"I had their chicken pot pie. It was yummy." She paused. "It was such a shame about Richard. I didn't know him very well, but he seemed like a nice man. He was very nice to Mom."

Wanda sniffed. "He was a nice man. I miss him."

"What's his daughter's name?" Elizabeth picked up a celery stick.

"Kathy. She teaches high school English." Wanda took a ladylike sip of her wine. "She and Richard didn't get on very well. He thought she should have gone into a career where she could make more money."

"Maybe teaching brings her joy. I think teachers are undervalued."

I reached for a carrot. "If anyone wants to eat tonight, I better get the salmon started." I stood.

Rob asked, "Do you need help?"

"No, it will only take a few minutes. Jenny, would you please set the table?"

She launched herself off the hearth. "Sure thing."

Jenny gathered plates, and I placed the salmon on a large piece of aluminum foil. I dressed it with a sauce of garlic, mustard, and white wine and closed the package by crimping the edges. I put it on a sheet pan, slid it into the oven, and set the timer. Then I brought water glasses to Jenny. "How long are you planning on staying at Cindy's?"

She paused, one of the forks still in her hand. "As long as Rob's mother is here if the Twilliger's will let me."

"I have a favor to ask."

"What?" She placed the fork on the left-hand side of the plate.

"Richard's daughter is coming to town for his funeral. Would it be okay if she stayed in your room?"

"All my stuff is there."

"I know. But you're not sleeping there, and the only other place is the couch. That's not very comfortable for a guest."

"I want all these people to go home!"

"Keep your voice down. They won't be here for that much longer. If there's anything you don't want Kathy to have access to, you can store it in my closet."

Jenny put the last knife down. "I guess. I'm not happy about it though."

I kissed her cheek. "Thanks."

Rob walked into the room. "Anything I can do?"

"You could fill the water pitcher and put it on the table."

Elizabeth came in with the plate we had used for hors d'oeuvres. "Where's your plastic wrap? I'll pop this into the fridge."

I pointed to the drawer to the left of the sink. "In there."

Rob took the containers of side dishes out of the refrigerator. "We're not going to put these onto serving plates, are we?"

Elizabeth laughed. "Fancy enough for me."

Wanda pointed to the containers. "Those are the end of civilization as we know it."

Rob refilled his mother's glass. "A bit dire. They aren't even plastic; they're made out of cardboard."

She took the glass from him and sipped. "I wasn't talking about garbage in the ocean. I was talking about how informal we as a society have become."

I pulled the tray from the oven. "Let's eat!"

After dinner, Wanda complained of a headache and went to bed early, and Jenny took some clothes and went back to Cindy's. Rob, Elizabeth, and I cleaned up.

Rob said to Elizabeth, "I have to cover the town council meeting tonight. Do you want to go back to my place, or would you rather stay here, and I'll pick you up on my way home?"

Elizabeth turned to me with a raised eyebrow.

"You're welcome to stay. I want the chance to get to know you better, and I think it's going to get pretty crazy after tonight."

She said, "I'll stay." Rob left.

I held the carafe. "More coffee?"

"No. I want to be able to sleep tonight. You don't have any Bailey's in the house, do you?"

I smiled. "You bet."

I retrieved the bottle and poured two cordial glasses. "Shall we return to the living room?" I led the way. We sat next to each other on the sofa.

She took a small sip and gave me an impish grin. "What deep dark secrets about Rob would you like to know? Let me see, how about the time he was caught skinny dipping in the lake—no that's too tame. There was the time the police brought him home after he snuck out his window." She chuckled. "He was five at the time and loved to explore. Still does."

I tucked one foot underneath me and leaned back onto the sofa. "All of those sound good. But Richard dying made me realize how little I know about your father. Rob never really talks about him."

She sat forward. "It was twenty years ago. It still seems so fresh."

"You don't have to talk about it if it makes you uncomfortable."

"It's okay. My dad was a journalist too. Mom didn't work outside the home, so they had difficulty making ends meet. We lived in the poorer section of town, but we had fun. We really did. There was so much love." She gave me a sad smile. "Rob followed in Dad's footsteps. Rob was in his last year of college, and I was in my last year of med school. Dad was investigating a series of pipe bombing incidents in the town next to us. I guess he got too close to the person responsible because they put one in his car."

Elizabeth rubbed her neck. "Mom was never the same. She never finished school—Dad swept her off her feet—so she felt unqualified for the jobs in which she was interested. She panicked and decided that she needed economic stability. Kind of like Scarlett O'Hara in Gone with the Wind. That began her long string of marital conquests, each leaving her more wealthy, but as far as I know, not happier." She took a sip of her drink. "I'm sorry. We were talking about Rob, and here I am bending your ear about Mom."

"I'm curious about something. You and your mom seem much closer than her and Rob."

She sighed. "Rob looks so much like Dad. Especially now that he's older, I think it's difficult for her. She was disappointed when he followed in Dad's footsteps, and her distance might be because she's worried she'll lose him too. It was worse when he was reporting from war zones."

"It's sad they're not closer. I was very close to both my parents. When my mother died, my father and I became even tighter. I still can't believe they're both gone. And so young."

"How did they die?"

"My mother had a rare form of cancer. She fought so bravely, but it ultimately claimed her. Dad was hit by a drunk driver two years later. They were both such loving people. It's been ten years since Dad died. I still miss them every day."

Elizabeth hugged me. "I'm so sorry."

I straightened my shoulders. "Enough about me. Richard's death must have been a shock."

"They're both older. And I didn't know him that well. I hope she waits a while before the next one."

My mouth dropped. "Surely you don't think that she would be looking for someone this soon."

"It seems to be her pattern." Elizabeth drank the rest of her Bailey's.

* * *

Work was crazy the next day. I ran home at lunch to change the sheets in Jenny's room and to run the vacuum cleaner. Checking that off my list, I grabbed a quick sandwich and headed back to work. Knee deep in a spreadsheet, I jumped when Cheryl knocked. She slid through the door and shut it behind her. "My sister-in-law called."

"And?"

"She heard Detective Ziebold talking with some of the other police officers." Cheryl sat. "Wanda's husband was poisoned."

I jerked back in my chair. "What? With what? When?"

Cheryl scooted her seat closer to my desk. "She didn't know. But they were talking about arresting Wanda."

Grabbing my phone, I pressed speed dial for Rob and gestured for Cheryl to shut the door after her.

"Hello, sunshine. How's your day going?"

I filled him in.

"She can't have done it—" He paused. "Gotta go, I'll talk to you later." Rob hung up.

I paced from one wall to the next. On my third turn, I pulled my purse from my desk and walked out of my office. "I'll be at home if you need me." I nodded at Cheryl and hurried out the door.

Walking fast, I made it home in record time. I swung open the back door. "Anyone here?" Nothing. I ran up the stairs, "Wanda?" No one.

I pulled out my trusty dust rag and cleaned the bookshelves in the living room. I had started on the mantle when there was a knock at the back door. Rob called, "Merry, you home?"

I ran into the kitchen. "What happened?"

Rob and Elizabeth dropped their coats on the kitchen stool. They both looked exhausted. Elizabeth sank onto one of the kitchen chairs. "They arrested Mom. Like she could kill anyone."

I sat next to her. "How did Richard die?"

Rob turned on the coffee machine. "They did a preliminary test. It came back positive for ricin poisoning. They've sent a sample out for confirmation."

"Confirmation—so he might not have been poisoned?"

Elizabeth shook her head. "The preliminary tests are usually accurate."

"Maybe it was in their motel room? Maybe that's where he was exposed."

Rob poured coffee into three mugs. "There would have been more cases at the motel by now. They think it was in the Prosecco."

Rob handed Elizabeth and me a mug. Steam rose in a tiny swirl. I blew on the coffee and then took a sip. Rob slumped onto a chair across from Elizabeth. "Mother said that Richard poured the champagne into the glasses. If that's true, it would have been difficult for her to pull off."

Elizabeth's mouth dropped. "You don't think she really did it, do you?"

He shook his head. "Of course not. But she's the only one he knew in town. Who else would have a motive?"

"Maybe it was a random thing?" Elizabeth stirred cream into her coffee.

"How would she even get ricin? It's not like she could send away for it." I leaned back in the chair.

"It's from the castor bean plant. The hulls contain ricin. Castor oil comes from the seeds, but only after the hulls have been removed." Elizabeth drank her coffee.

Rob gave his sister a sidelong glance. "It's a good thing you weren't here when Richard died."

She shrugged. "Learned about it in medical school." Her eyes flicked to me. "At any rate, Mom's lawyer is with her now."

My eyes widened. "I can't imagine her spending the night in jail. Hopefully, he'll be able to get them to set bail quickly." I drummed my fingers on the kitchen table. "Richard's daughter is supposed to come on Saturday. I wonder how she's going to feel, staying in the same house as the woman accused of her father's murder."

CHAPTER 4

The doorbell rang at ten, and I hurried to open it. A carefully put together woman of about fifty was on my porch. She wore a brown tweed skirt, chocolate-colored flats, and a crisp white shirt with a princess collar. Her cardigan rested on her arm. I held out my hand. "Kathy?"

"Yes. Merry?"

"Welcome." I ushered her into the house. "I am so sorry about your father's passing."

"Thank you." She lifted a small carry-on and brought it in with her.

"Would you like to freshen up?"

She nodded.

I led her up the stairs and ushered her into Jenny's room. "I've cleaned out the top drawer and made some hanging room in the closet if you'd like to use it."

She dropped her case in the room.

"The bathroom is down here." I pointed it out. "If there's anything you forgot to bring, let me know."

I walked down the stairs, made my way into the kitchen, and turned on the coffee pot. I cut the freshly made crumb cake into small pieces and arrayed them on a plate.

Kathy walked into the kitchen. "That looks good."

"I thought you might want something to eat. I know they don't give you anything in the way of food on planes these days. Would you like coffee or tea?"

"Coffee's fine. Cream and sugar if you have it."

I poured her a mug and slid it across the counter. I picked up mine and the crumb cake and sat next to her.

She helped herself to a piece and took a bite. "Thank you for going to all this trouble. I feel like I should be doing something, but my dad and I weren't close, and I hardly know Wanda—I think we've only spoken on the phone once or twice." She looked at the ceiling. "They've only been married for a year or two. They had one of those destination weddings in Fiji." She sipped her coffee. "It didn't seem worth it to go. It was my Dad's sixth marriage; I stopped going after the second one.

"You never really know how long you'll have with someone. I should have stayed in touch—made more of an effort." A tear rolled down her face. She swiped at it. "I don't know why I'm getting so sentimental. I said goodbye to him a long time ago."

I poured her more coffee.

She looked me in the eyes. "It was a man, of course. I was madly in love. My dad didn't think he was good enough for me. He paid him off." She sighed. "I guess if he could be bought off, my dad was probably right. But at the time, I thought he ruined my life forever." She played with her napkin. "And maybe he did. Look at me. Not married, no kids."

"I'm sorry you've had such a tough time."

She pulled my notebook to her. "Enough about that. Why don't you show me what you have planned?"

I took her through the Mass, the catering, and the people I thought would attend.

"You've thought of everything. I even like the readings you selected."

"Would you like to read one."

"I would. I'll do this one, Acts 10:34-43. I like how it ends '...Everyone who believes in Him will receive forgiveness of sins.' I think he believed, and he certainly had a lot of sins that needed to be forgiven."

My eyes widened.

The back door opened, and Wanda strolled in. She was wearing a black Chanel suit with what looked to be a very expensive brooch. She walked forward, her hand out. "You must be Kathy. I'm Wanda. I'm sorry we've only ever spoken on the phone. Your father admired you so much."

Kathy stood and backed away. "I thought you'd still be in jail."

"I got out on bail late last night."

"The police have been giving me updates. They said you poisoned him."

Wanda closed the gap between them. "I didn't. I wouldn't even know how to find—"

"Ricin."

"That's right. How would I know where to get something like that?"

Kathy sank back onto her chair. "I don't even know you. I don't know how I'm supposed to believe you. My lawyer said that you're getting everything—" She stood abruptly. "This was a mistake. I'll find a motel."

I rose. "I can understand how you feel, but the only place near town isn't appropriate. Why don't you go up to your room and rest, and we'll see what we can work out?"

She trudged up the steps and shut her door.

Wanda said, "I can't believe she would think—I would never do anything like that. No matter how much money was involved."

I bit my lip. "Kathy seems pretty upset. I think we're going to have to make other arrangements until you are cleared of the murder, or she goes back home."

"You're not suggesting I leave?"

"We need to do some shuffling. At least in the short term."

"I'll be in my room." She stormed up the steps.

I called Rob. "Need you to intervene. Kathy doesn't want to stay in the same house as your mother."

"I'll be there in a few minutes."

I collapsed onto the chair. *Houseguests.*

Rob walked in with Elizabeth ten minutes later. "Where's Mother?"

I pointed up. He kissed the top of my head and ran up the stairs. A door opened and shut.

Elizabeth poured a cup of coffee. "I'm sorry for all this bother."

"Not your fault. We'll get through this."

A few minutes later, Rob returned. "She's packing. She's not happy, but at least she's leaving." He went to get her suitcase, and then they came back down the steps.

Wanda nodded to Elizabeth and then walked out the door without looking at me.

Rob trailed. "Sorry. I'll talk to you later."

I put my coffee cup down. "I'll be back in a few minutes." I strode up the steps and knocked softly on Kathy's door.

"Come in."

I shut the door behind me. She lay on the bed reading; a quilt tucked around her. I said, "We're going to move people around. Wanda is going to stay at her son's house, and her daughter is going to stay here. I want you to feel comfortable."

She put her book down and sat up. "It seems like an awful lot of trouble."

"We're all set. We'll have lunch at one if you feel up to it."

"Thank you." She curled up again, and I left.

I stripped the sheets from the guest bed and put on new ones. Elizabeth stood in the doorway. "I could have done that." She picked up one side of the quilt and helped me put it on the bed.

I smoothed an errant crease. "All done. Thanks for the assist." The clock chimed twelve. "Welcome to casa March."

She giggled. "It will be fun to have more time to get to know you."

"I'll let you put your things away. Come down when you're ready." I carried the sheets downstairs and put them in the wash.

Sitting at the kitchen counter, I finished making a list of the things needed from the store. Task accomplished, I doodled in the margins. *If Wanda didn't kill Richard, who did?*

Elizabeth came into the kitchen. "Can I help you set out lunch?"

"Yes, hopefully, you like tuna salad; I made a ton of it."

"You're in luck. It's my favorite."

"Since you're a surgeon, I'll let you slice the tomatoes." I handed her the knife. "Do you get that a lot?"

"What?"

"People expecting you to do the carving."

She chuckled. "Every day."

Kathy joined us. "Can I help?"

Elizabeth turned from where she was making precise cuts on the tomatoes. "I'd shake your hand but—" She waved the knife.

I handed Kathy the bowl of tuna salad. "Set the table?"

"Sure. I love tuna."

I finished washing the lettuce and put it on a plate lined with a paper towel. "What would you ladies like to drink with lunch? I have milk, sodas, or lemonade."

In unison, they said, "Milk."

"Milk it is." I poured three glasses and handed them to Kathy. She deposited them on the table.

"Anyone want chips?" Two heads nodded. I grabbed a bag and placed it on the table, along with the bread. Elizabeth brought over the tomatoes and lettuce, and we sat.

Elizabeth added an extra piece of lettuce to her sandwich and turned to Kathy. "I'm so sorry for your loss; it must be difficult for you."

Kathy shivered. "I can't believe he's dead. And poisoned. I was sure he'd get shot."

My eyes grew round. "I know you said he wasn't the nicest man in the world, but did you really think someone would shoot him?"

"Well he was in 'sanitation.'" Kathy motioned with air quotes.

"Why would that make someone want to kill him?" Elizabeth took a bite of her sandwich.

"I don't think she really meant he was in sanitation," I said.

Kathy pointed at me. "Bingo. That was his front. I heard some things. I think he was connected."

"What made you think that?"

"A man came to our house in Lancaster ages ago. I was playing hide and seek from the governess and ended up in a closet in my dad's office. The door was slightly ajar. My dad came around the desk and sat. I was very quiet and stared at him." She popped a potato chip in her mouth. "I wasn't allowed to be in there." She gave a thin smile. "That's what made it such a great hiding place.

"Anyway, a few minutes later, another man came in. I couldn't see him; he must have been across the desk. He begged my father to extend the time to pay back a loan. My dad slowly picked up the bat he had lying on the floor under his desk. He slapped it against his hand several times and said, 'If I give you extra time, Mrs. Thomas will want extra time, and then Mr. Duncan; pretty soon I'll be out of business. No. I want my money, and I want it by noon tomorrow.' He pointed the bat toward where the man must have been sitting and said, 'Understand?'

"I crawled to the back of the closet and waited for what seemed like an eternity. I finally heard my father's office door shut. I crawled to the opening and scanned the room. It was empty. I slid out, tiptoed to the door, and slowly opened it. I peered out. No one in the hallway. I jumped through the door and shut it behind me. That was the last time I used his closet as a hiding place."

Elizabeth leaned forward. "Do you think he was a loan shark?"

"I didn't know what he was, back then. I was too young. I understood more when I was older and saw some of his business practices. Being a loan shark was one of his businesses." She took another chip and lifted her eyes to mine. "The tuna salad was terrific. I like the fact that you chopped up bits of pickle into it. The brine is a nice offset to the richness of the mayo."

I sipped my milk. "That's quite a story. Did your father and mother get divorced?"

She pushed the lone remaining potato chip around her plate with her finger. "My mother disappeared when I was fourteen. I like to think she's living on a Caribbean Island somewhere."

"What did the police say?"

"They officially listed her as missing. Her passport was gone, along with some of her clothes. But I don't think she would have left me. She loved me."

Elizabeth sat back. "That's tragic. I'm so sorry to hear that."

"Thanks. It happened such a long time ago that sometimes I think I just dreamed I had a mother; that she was never really there."

I gulped. "Who's up for homemade chocolate chip cookies?"

Kathy raised her hand.

* * *

The church was half full for the Funeral Mass on Monday. I was happy with the attendance but exhausted. Patty and I had called many of the parishioners on Sunday, pleading with them to attend. It might have been easier to hire professional mourners. Rob sat with his mother and sister in the front pew on the left-hand side of the church, and

Jenny and I sat with Kathy on the right-hand side. Father Tom did an excellent job with the sermon, weaving in the remembrances and stories Wanda and Kathy had shared with him.

As we formed a receiving line, I was careful to put Kathy at the front, and Wanda at the end. Patty handed out small cards that invited mourners to my house after the burial. I was pleased to see my new neighbor as she left the church. "Alex, it's so kind of you to attend." I shook her hand.

"We're neighbors. Of course I came." She skirted the rest of the receiving line and left the church.

Two big men came out last. I sidled up to Rob as we walked to the gravesite. "Who were they?"

"Said they were business associates."

"Large guys."

"Wouldn't want to run into them in a dark alley."

"Nope."

We climbed the small hill to the burial site. Two heavy boards suspended the casket over the grave. Draping masked the opening that yawned underneath, but the aroma of freshly dug earth hung in the air. A small line of white folding chairs sat near the coffin, protected against the chance of inclement weather by the canopy above. Wanda sat on the chair furthest left and Kathy on the one furthest right. Rob, Elizabeth, Jenny, and I sat between them. Father Tom said a few words, and then we lined up to put roses on the casket. Once they had placed their flowers, Rob, Wanda, Elizabeth, and Jenny left for the house. Kathy was the last one to approach. Her lips moved as if she was praying silently, and then she rested her forehead on the coffin. I touched her shoulder. "Are you okay? Do you want some time alone?"

She lifted her head, wiping at her eyes. "I'm fine. Thanks."

"Let's go back to the house."

The street was lined with cars. I turned to Kathy. "It looks like people got here before us."

The kitchen was crowded, and Ed shouted over the din, "Good. You're back. I need more platters."

I strode past him and stretched to try and open the top cupboard. Rob appeared at my side. "What do you need?"

I pointed to the platters. He grabbed three and handed them to me. I said, "Must be nice to be tall."

He kissed the top of my head. "Makes me handy to have around."

I passed the platters to Ed. "What else do you need?"

He paused his plating. "Can you take the cheese puffs out of the oven? Andy's pouring wine in the living room."

"No problem." I opened the oven and was enveloped by the delightful aroma of melted cheddar cheese. My stomach growled. I looked over my shoulder. "How long do these have to cool?"

"Give them at least three minutes. You won't burn your mouth, and they'll taste better."

I set the timer. "What else?"

"I'm good for now. Go mingle."

I slid past people in the crowded hall, emerging in the living room. Andy had a bottle of white wine in one hand and a bottle of red in his left. I came up behind him. "I didn't know you were ambidextrous."

"You're finally here." He pointed with the top of the wine bottle at the Finnegans. "They want coffee. Could you make a pot?"

Rob walked into the living room, carrying a carafe of coffee. Andy blinked. "He's good. You should keep him around." Andy topped off another person's glass.

I retrieved coffee cups from the dining room and walked in front of Rob, handing out mugs, as he trailed behind me pouring the coffee. Richard's two business associates took up most of one corner. Their eyes roved the room, more intent on the crowd than each other. Patty appeared at my shoulder. "You may want to get to the kitchen. Kathy and Wanda are squaring off."

I handed her the two remaining mugs and wound my way back through the packed hallway into the kitchen. Wanda and Kathy stood a foot apart glaring at each other. People formed a circle around them, closely watching the drama playing out. I grabbed an antacid from the drawer and chewed it.

Wanda said, "He was so disappointed in you. He was hoping you'd take over the family business."

Kathy grimaced. "The family business? Not likely. Wouldn't you like to know where his money came from? I chose an honorable profession."

"He was a businessman. There wasn't anything wrong with his company."

"Whatever." Kathy flicked her hand dismissively.

"You should thank me. I made your father happy."

"You were one in a long line of floozies. It was only a matter of time before he showed you the door." Kathy lifted the wine glass to her lips.

"How would you know? You never talked to him."

"The house staff. They practically raised me, you know." Kathy smirked, turned her back, and walked away.

Wanda paled and swayed. I grabbed her arm to steady her. "Are you okay?" I motioned for the crowd to give us room, pulled a chair out from the table, and put her in it.

Elizabeth joined me. "Mom, take a breath. That's it. Nice and easy."

Wanda began to regain some color. "I want to go back to Rob's. Now."

"I'll get his keys." Elizabeth walked back down the hall.

I crouched next to Wanda. "Would you rather lie down in my room?"

She glared at me. "I don't want to spend another moment under the same roof as that woman."

Elizabeth handed her mother her purse. "Let's go. Do you need help?"

Her mother shrugged her off and pushed through the crowd for the door, like a salmon swimming upstream in the spawning season.

* * *

The dishwasher was on its third load, and Rob and I sprawled in the living room. I nudged him. "A little more wine please." He topped off my glass. I lifted it. "To the funeral being over."

Rob said, "Amen to that."

Kathy strolled down the steps. "May I join you?"

"Certainly." I pointed to an open chair. "Would you like some wine?"

She nodded, and Rob poured her a glass. "I'm sorry I spoke harshly to your mother. It was kind of you to plan this for my father, and I made a scene." She sipped the wine.

"It was an emotional day. Did you try one of Ed's cheese puffs? They're cold now, but they're still delicious." I pushed the tray toward her.

"Thanks. I didn't get a chance to eat much."

"Would you like me to make you a sandwich?"

"No." She gestured toward the coffee table. "I'll pick at what's left." She selected a carrot stick and dipped it in the roasted red pepper hummus. "Did Ed make the dip?"

"Yes."

She bit into the carrot and slowly chewed. "It's so good."

"It's too bad you're leaving tomorrow. I'd take you to his tea room.

"Did you see the two goons?" She popped another cheese puff in her mouth.

Rob put his wine glass down. "Yes. Business acquaintances of your dad's?"

She snorted. "They were his muscle. The people he sent when he wanted to keep other people in line."

My jaw dropped. "They were his enforcers?"

"Pretty much. And if they showed up here, they must be trying to find out who killed Richard." She patted her lips with a napkin. "Your mother's been charged. Maybe they think she didn't do it."

Rob stood. "Speaking of my mother, I should be getting back." He turned to Kathy. "What time is your flight tomorrow?"

"Early. The car's picking me up at six."

He shook her hand. "It was good to meet you."

"Same."

I rose. "I'll walk you out."

We stood by his car, and he hugged me. "It feels like we haven't been alone in weeks."

"We haven't."

"One kiss." His lips met mine.

Still smiling, I let myself back in the front door. Kathy said, "He seems like a nice man."

"He is." I sat on the couch and tucked my foot underneath me. "How did you know those two men were your father's enforcers?"

"Easy. When I was sixteen, my father told me I couldn't go out with my boyfriend one night. I was bored and pissed off. So when the phone rang, I picked it up at the same time as him. My father told Frank, the one with brown hair and the scar, to take care of the Peabodys. A week later the newspaper reported that some people named Peabody had lost control of their car on a turn. At first, they thought it was an accident because the guy was going pretty fast. But then they found out their brake lines had been cut. I probably should have gone to the police. But I was a kid; who would have listened to me?" She crossed her arms. "I told you he wasn't a very nice man."

CHAPTER 5

I wiped away the last of the water rings that somehow ended up on every surface downstairs after having gotten up early to see Kathy off. Soon everyone would go home, and my house would return to normal.

I made fresh coffee, and Elizabeth rounded the corner into the kitchen. She pointed at the pot. "Is that for me?"

I filled a mug and handed it to her. "I have some leftover coffee cake if you'd like it."

She mumbled something that I took to be a yes. I heated a piece in the microwave for a few seconds and brought it over to her.

"Thanks." She yawned. "Rob, Mom, and I were playing cards last night until late."

"How was she?"

"Still shaken up." Elizabeth used the side of her fork to cut a piece of the cake.

"I can see how that would be upsetting."

"By the time I left, she seemed okay. She was talking about firing his staff and selling the house. She said it was a monstrosity. She showed me a picture, and she's not wrong."

"I wonder if Kathy has any affection for the house. Maybe Wanda should see if she wants to buy it."

Elizabeth paused. "I don't think she'd be able to afford it on a teacher's salary. Plus it's quite a distance from where she works."

"It's sad. I think it was their family home. She even kept up with the house staff."

"My mother won't listen to me when it comes to money." Elizabeth shifted in her seat. "I'm worried about leaving tomorrow with Mom still under suspicion for Richard's murder, but I've patients waiting for me."

"Rob and I will look out for her. If anything changes, we're only a short flight away."

She stood. "I'd better let you get to work. I'll cook dinner tonight."

"You're on." I tossed her my keys. "In case you need something from the store."

Strolling to work, I texted Jenny. "Are you coming home today? Bedroom's back to normal. It would be nice if you came for dinner. Elizabeth's last night."

"Okay."

I sighed. It would be nice to have Jenny back home. I missed hearing about her school day, her hugs, and the sound of her voice. I hurried to work, and the day was hectic from the moment I set foot inside the office. We still had quite a few claims pending after the storm, and the people who hadn't sustained damage were calling to double-check their coverage. The staff did a good job coping with both, but there were some calls I needed to handle. At six, I wrapped up the last of the paperwork and made my way home.

It was a lovely spring day, and the sun still seemed high in the sky. My tight shoulders relaxed. People were planting pansies of all different hues. I walked through my gate and swore that I would fill my planters soon. I opened the back door, and the mouthwatering smell of garlic, tomatoes, and onions wafted toward me. I put my briefcase on the floor and my purse on the kitchen stool. "Smells terrific. Why haven't I had you cook before?"

Elizabeth stirred the mixture in the sauté pan. "It's my take on chicken cacciatore." She poured red wine to deglaze the pan and then nestled the chicken amongst the mushrooms and peppers. She handed me the bottle. "Pour yourself a glass. I got it from your local wine shop."

I chuckled. "Your mother thought the Pick of the Vine was provincial."

She rolled her eyes. "Mom wouldn't know a good wine if it bit her."

"What can I do to help?"

"Salad fixings are in the fridge. You could toss those together in a bowl. We'll be eating in about thirty minutes. Jenny's upstairs."

I got to work, and a few moments later there was a knock at the back door. Rob and his mother walked in, deep in conversation. She said, "I still don't understand why I have to stay here in town. They should accept my word that I'll come back if and when they have a trial."

Elizabeth stirred fresh peas into the rice. "You've been charged with murder, and you live in a different state. They are not going to let you leave."

"That's what I keep trying to tell her." Rob's normally sparkly green eyes had bags under them. He kissed my cheek. "What can I do?"

His mother sat at the table. "You could pour me a glass of wine to start."

"I was talking to Merry." He spat each word.

"I'll get your mother a glass of wine; you set the table." I touched his arm.

He flashed me a quick smile and gathered plates.

I poured Wanda a glass of white wine and brought it to her. "Elizabeth was kind enough to cook tonight. Hopefully, we can find something more pleasant to talk about."

"I don't know why she gets to go home, and I don't. I didn't kill Richard. No matter what his daughter says." Wanda set her glass down on the table.

I leaned against the kitchen counter. "Actually, the last thing Kathy said to me was that she thought you might not have done it."

Elizabeth's eyebrow rose. "How did she come to this epiphany?"

"Because Richard's business associates turned up. I wonder if they're still in town."

* * *

Rob took his sister to the airport. I hurried to work, crossing my fingers that it would be a slower day. Thank heavens, it was. Cheryl came in with my call list. "You have some catching up to do if you want to make all your outbound calls this week."

"I may give myself some leeway. I think between the funeral and the storm, I've spoken to everyone in town. Do you have a moment?"

She said, "Sure," and sat down.

"Is your cousin still a maid at the motel?"

"Yes. She's been thinking of another line of work though. She says it creeps her out that someone was murdered there."

"I can see how it might." I tapped my pencil on the desk. "Two men came to the funeral. They were big, and one had a jagged scar running down the right side of his face. Would you check with her to see if they are staying there?"

"No problem." She stood. "Anything else?"

"Yes. Would you call Patty, and find out if she's free for lunch?" I held up the list. "I need to get busy."

Twenty minutes later, Cheryl stuck her head in the door. "Patty's good for lunch at Delightful Bites at noon, and my cousin said your mystery men are staying at the motel. They haven't checked out yet."

I doodled for a moment and then picked up the phone to continue my calls. The alarm rang, giving me ten minutes to get to lunch, so I gave my lips a quick swipe with gloss and walked out the door. Patty was standing in line when I got there. She ordered and claimed a table, and a few minutes later, I joined her. "You are such a good friend. Thank you for helping with the funeral. I couldn't have done it without you."

"No, you couldn't." She sipped her coffee. "Has everyone gone home now?"

I groaned. "Everyone except for Wanda. She has to stay in town until the trial. Or until I kill her."

"Don't say that so loud."

"I'm not sure I care. I liked Rob's sister; she's great. But his mother is another thing entirely. I guess I have some sympathy for her, losing Rob's father in such a violent way. But still."

"She must be pushing your buttons. You don't normally talk trash about anyone."

I sat straighter. "You're right. I should keep my feelings to myself."

Patty touched my shoulder. "It's okay. I'm a haven. I'm not going to tell anyone. Now, why are we having lunch?"

"The tough guys from the funeral are staying at our local 'no-tell' motel."

"And this concerns me why?" Patty lifted her sandwich to her lips.

"I want to find out why they're still here."

"Maybe they like to shop for antiques."

I put my spoon down. "Did they look like doily shoppers to you?"

She smirked. "Nope. Maybe machine guns."

"I thought we might follow them to see what they're up to."

She set her coffee down. "You want us to follow two goons by ourselves?"

I nodded. "I want to see where they go. Wine at my house afterward. I'll pick you up at seven."

* * *

I eased the car into a parking spot with a good view of the door and shut off the headlights. "May as well get comfortable. We may be here a while."

"I shouldn't have had that extra glass of water at dinner," Patty said. "How much longer are we going to be here?"

"Wimp. There's a bathroom past the front desk. I'm sure if you ask nicely, they'll let you use it."

Patty eased open the door while I covered the car light with my purse.

I hissed, "Hurry back."

She scurried to the door, pushed it open, and passed the two men we were supposed to be following. Patty disappeared into the motel. The two men walked to a large black Lincoln and slid in. The car purred as it passed me moving toward the exit. I stared daggers at the motel door. "C'mon Patty. Where the heck are you?"

She darted out the door, running full tilt toward the car. I pulled up next to her. "Get in." Patty jumped into the car, and I floored it. "Didn't you see them come out?"

"Of course. They held the door for me."

"I'm happy they still have their manners. They took a left on Lemon. Hold on." My tires squealed, and I made a sharp turn. I pointed to a car stopped at the traffic light. "You're lucky they were going slow." I stopped behind them. The light changed, and the men proceeded at a slow pace toward the center of town. "Where do you think they're going?"

"Late dinner?"

The Lincoln pulled into the parking lot of the Pickled Herring and backed into a spot against the building. I turned to Patty. "I guess they like to make quick exits."

"What are we going to do?"

"Let's wait for a few minutes, and if they don't come out, we'll go in and have a drink at the bar."

"You're paying."

I backed into a space toward the end of the lot. Patty looked at me. I huffed, "It doesn't hurt to be prepared."

The car was facing the town square. Patty squealed, "Look. The tulips will be blooming soon."

There was a large garden dominating the open space. Volunteers from the chamber of commerce took turns, keeping it looking pristine. When the tulips bloomed, they spelled out Hopeful, the name of our town. "They're going to be so pretty this year. I heard they went with strong reds. Along with the bright pink azaleas, they'll look perfect."

"I love this time of year." The car's clock ticked forward. "They've been in there five minutes. I don't think they're coming out any time soon. Let's go. We'll sit on the side of the bar facing them. It doesn't look like that many people are here."

Patty muscled the heavy door open. "I love the look of these old doors, but they're a work-out."

I led the way into the dimly lit room. A large oval bar dominated the space, with gleaming mahogany counters. Our subjects sat on the right side of the bar. There were some seats on the left, so Patty and I climbed onto the bar stools. The bartender, Ann, was waiting on another customer, she served him a drink, and then came our way. "Hello, ladies. What can I bring you?"

Patty said, "Merlot."

I nodded. "Same."

Ann poured two glasses and placed them in front of us. Then she went to the end of the bar and picked up two sandwiches. She set them in front of our quarry.

Patty said, "Eating late."

"Looks that way." I motioned for Ann.

She came back. "What's up? Is the wine off?"

I shook my head. "No, but I would appreciate a glass of water."

Patty held up two fingers. Ann bent over for the soda hose. She dipped two glasses into the ice bin and pressed the water button. "Anything else?"

I whispered, "Who are your two new friends?" She started to look over her shoulder. I touched her arm. "Don't look."

"You mean the new guys on the other side of the bar?"

I gave her a thumbs up.

"The guy with the scar is Frank. His friend goes by Bud. They wanted to know if there were any new people in town."

"What did you tell them?"

"I mentioned Rob's mother and her late husband—" she leaned closer—"They said they knew him. There's also your new neighbor, the guy and his wife who moved into that house on Elm, and two sisters who are renting a house on Crescent. I told them I didn't know everyone, but those were the people I could remember."

"Who bought the one on Elm? Was it the craftsman?"

"A nice older couple. They came in the other day for sherry. It's the gray house with the large square pillars." She shined the top of the bar in front of us.

"I'll need to introduce myself."

Patty elbowed me. "Let's keep on task, shall we?" She turned to Ann. "Did they say why they wanted to know?"

"They said they were thinking of moving here and wanted to make sure it wasn't one of those transient towns where people continually move in and out. They want to have some permanence."

Patty rolled her eyes. "Sure they do."

A customer at the end of the bar raised his glass. Ann picked up her rag. "Gotta go."

"What's next?" Patty rolled and unrolled her paper napkin.

"I don't know. We could relax and finish our wine."

Ann stood back in front of us. "The gentlemen over there would like to buy you two a drink." She moved to one side, and the goons waved at us.

Patty lifted her left hand, pointed to her wedding ring, and mouthed, "Sorry."

They both turned to me. My face grew hot. I gave a quick shake of my head and studied the bar top.

Ann said, "I guess that's a no. I thought it might be." She grinned and turned on her heel.

I put money on the bar and stood. "Let's go."

We slunk to the car. Patty laughed. "We were so inconspicuous that our targets offered to buy us a drink. I guess we shouldn't plan on following anyone else."

I got into the car. "That was embarrassing. Although to look on the bright side, we haven't lost it."

"What's next? Are we going to continue to follow them?"

"No. I'll drop you home. I think it's time to have a little talk with my favorite detective."

CHAPTER 6

Saturday morning, I stretched and then began my cleaning routine. I started with my bathroom upstairs and worked my way from there. The vacuum cleaner accidentally bumped Jenny's door. She swung it open. "Can't a person get some sleep around here?"

"It's ten. You should be up."

"Read the articles, Mom. Teens need sleep." She slammed the door. Feeling guilty, I left the vacuum in the hall and went downstairs to dust. I moved methodically, yet quietly, my routine well established. My phone dinged with a text from Jay. "Can meet you at two. Your place."

I put the dust cloth away and hurried into the kitchen. I set butter out to soften and assembled everything I needed for chocolate chip cookies. In the middle of mixing them, there was a knock at the back door. Rob walked in and gave me a big hug. "You're a sight for sore eyes."

I looked behind him. "Where's your mother?"

"She went shopping, thank God. I needed a break. I love her, but she drives me crazy."

"Uh-huh." I kissed him.

"Making cookies?"

"Yes. Jay's coming over at two." I formed the cookies and placed them on the baking sheet.

"Those aren't all for him, are they?"

I smiled. "There may be one or two left for you."

"Why is he coming over?"

"Can you wait? I'll rather tell you both at the same time. Did you have lunch?"

"Not yet. Do you want to go out?"

I shook my head. "I stocked up. Deli meat is in the fridge." I put out bread, lettuce, tomatoes, and condiments. "Soda?" He nodded, so I poured him a cola.

Jenny walked into the kitchen. "Lunch? Can't we have breakfast?"

"Breakfast was hours ago. Have lunch with us, or make yourself something." I put the cookies in the oven and sat at the kitchen table.

Rob joined me. "Jenny, what kind of sandwich would you like?"

"Roast beef, I guess. Is there Swiss cheese?"

"Yes."

"Lettuce, tomato, and mayo, please." He handed her the finished product. She inspected it. "Looks good. Thanks." She hopped up and retrieved chips. "My birthday's coming up."

I paused, mid-bite. "Your birthday's not until August. You still have a few months."

She picked up a chip. "I thought it would be nice to have a car for my last year of high school."

"The high school isn't that far away. It's better to stretch your legs and walk after sitting all day in class."

"Dad gave me a car."

Rob put his sandwich down. "Your father gave you a car that he bought with the money he swindled from other people. That's why the FBI seized it."

I rubbed my neck. "Don't remind me."

"At least I got to drive it once before they took it. I loved that car. Fire engine red. So hot." She sat back in her seat. The timer rang. "I'll check the cookies."

Jenny took the cookies out of the oven and put the tray on a cooling rack. "Anyway, it would be good to have a car."

"I'll think about it. Don't forget you may not be able to have a car as a freshman on some campuses."

"That's more than a year away. And it's something I can put on my criteria sheet for where I want to go."

Rob asked, "Criteria sheet?"

Jenny held up the milk jug. "Anyone?" We both nodded, so she filled three glasses. She put several cookies on a plate and brought them over. "I'm listing out the most important things I'm looking for in a school. That way I'll be able to cross-reference and compare the various schools."

He leaned forward. "What's on your list?"

"The typical stuff. Large school, small school, how close it is to home, if they specialize in something. That kind of thing."

"Sounds thorough. I'm impressed."

I interjected, "It's becoming quite the spreadsheet. She even has pivot tables."

"Well if you decide to get her a car, I'd be happy to help her pick it out."

"Don't you start."

Jenny stood and carried the plates to the sink. "I'm going to the park with Jacob. I'll be back at five." She stopped by Rob's chair. "Thanks for the sandwich and for being on my side about the car."

He opened his mouth, and she trotted out the back door. He turned to me. "I hope you know I wasn't taking sides."

"I know." I rubbed his shoulder. "But next time don't be so helpful."

"Okay." He ate another cookie. "What time are we supposed to be at Ed and Andy's tonight?"

"Six."

"Thanks for asking them to invite my mother. I didn't want to leave her alone."

"Let's hope they're still talking to us tomorrow." I slapped my hand across my mouth. "Did I say that out loud?"

He laughed. "Yes, you did. And I completely understand. This situation has been stressful for all of us, Mother included."

The door opened, and Jay walked in. "Oh, good. Chocolate chip. My favorite." He glared at the empty carafe. "No coffee?"

Rob leaped up. "Ready in a few."

Jay sat at the table. "Now what was it you wanted to tell me about?"

"Do you remember the two huge guys from the funeral?"

"Yeah. One guy had an ugly scar on his face."

"They're still in town, staying at the motel."

He broke his chocolate chip cookie in two, and gooey strands of chocolate drooped. "These are great. Love homemade." He lifted his eyes to mine. "Maybe they like antiques."

Rob poured the coffee. "Doubtful."

"Maybe they like opera too. Takes all kinds." Jay sat back in his chair and shook his finger at me. "I know where you are going with this. You're going to tell me that they murdered Richard."

I shook my head. "As far as I know, they weren't in town yet. Kathy told me they worked for her father. Richard's dying means they're out of a job. I think they're trying to figure out who killed Richard."

Jay stood. "We know who killed Richard. It was his wife. She inherits everything. And from what I've found out, that's a lot. Somewhere north of ten mill."

Rob's mouth dropped. "That much?"

I sipped my coffee. "And she didn't want to pay anything for catering."

"We've got the right person. I'm sorry that it's your mom." He nodded at Rob and left.

Rob stood and then sat back down as if he were tethered to the chair by a bungee cord. He whispered, "She didn't let on that it was quite so much. I wonder if she knew."

I placed my hand on top of his. "It's a lot to take in."

"I can't believe she killed him. My mother would never do that. But she's changed so much. Do I really know her anymore?" His green eyes studied mine.

"People don't change that much." I stood and hugged him.

He put his arms around me. "The money gives her a heck of a motive."

* * *

Andy and Ed's welcome party for Alex was in full swing when we got there. It was a balmy spring night, and the wide French doors to their back deck stood open to allow for better crowd flow. Rob, Wanda, and I scooted up the steps. I carried a chicken tetrazzini casserole, Rob had two bottles of wine, and Wanda a salad. I cut a path through the crowd to the kitchen. Ed gestured like an air traffic controller, instructing people where to put the food they brought. The kitchen island was draped with a sky blue cloth and white pedestals of varying heights, which displayed the potluck offerings for the evening. He waved me closer. "Put your hot dish over here—Wanda, is that a salad?"

Her eyes widened at the commotion in the room. She stopped in her tracks. I placed my dish where instructed and turned to take the salad. "Here, Wanda. Let me." I reached for the bowl.

She let it go. "All this food."

I put the salad down. "Let's try to make our way into the living room." We squirmed through the various cliques that had formed. I introduced Wanda to several people, and at last, we found a spot near Patrick and Patty that wasn't quite as congested. Rob wound his way to us, holding the wine glasses up over the fray.

Patty said, "It's nice that so many people turned out to meet Alex. Where is she, by the way?"

I pointed toward the kitchen. "Over there. I'll try to talk to her later. I guess we should have gotten here earlier."

"I'm not sure why we had to come at all. We could have had a nice quiet dinner on our own." Wanda slid onto a chair someone had vacated for her.

Rob handed her a glass of white wine. "If you get tired, you can always go back to Merry's. She'll give you the key."

Ed rang the dinner bell. "This is going to take some maneuvering, but the food is ready. Come when you want."

Several people strode toward the kitchen. I caught Rob's eye. "Let's wait for the frenzy to subside."

Alex walked toward us. "Whew. That kitchen is packed. Hope the fire marshal isn't here!"

I moved forward. "I don't think you've met my boyfriend, Rob." He held out his hand, and she shook it. "This is his mother, Wanda."

She waved. Wanda studied her. "You look so familiar. Have we met?"

Alex shook her head. "I don't think so."

"I'm sure I know you from somewhere."

"I guess I have one of those faces."

Rob broke in, "Merry tells me you're an artist. She said you do landscapes."

"Yes. I love to paint. And this town has so many inspirational places."

Patrick chimed in, "Have you been to the oriental garden yet?"

"Where is that?"

"Just a short drive from town. I'd be happy to show you one day."

Wanda prodded me with her finger. "The line looks like it's going down." She stood. I gestured for Rob to take the lead.

"We're going to get in line if anyone would care to join us."

Alex said, "I'm going to mingle a bit longer."

"Lead the way," Patty got in line behind me, and Patrick brought up the rear.

As we entered the kitchen, Ed gestured for Wanda to go on one side of the island and Rob the other. "Everything looks so good," I said. Ed moved me along.

Plates full, Andy waved us to a table that had been vacated outside. "There are five seats here."

Rob moved past Andy. "You and Ed are so efficient. When are you going to eat?"

He sighed. "When we get most of the people through. Have you seen Alex?"

"She was in the living room. She said she'd be out later."

"She's a regular social butterfly." Two more people came out of the back door. He waved. "Over here. Someone can sit at the table, and the other person can sit on the step."

✳ ✳ ✳

Rob and I collapsed on the sofa in my living room. "So many people," I sighed.

"It was fun though."

"All except the part where your mom spit out Mary Jessup's pie."

"In her defense, Mary had confused the salt for the sugar."

"It would have been nicer if she hadn't demanded to know who made it."

"No argument here. Bailey's?" He stood and strolled toward the liquor cabinet.

"Would love some. Too bad the glasses are so tiny."

His eyebrow arched. "I could get you a larger glass."

"Kidding."

He sank onto the couch and pulled me close. "It sounds wrong to say this, but I'm glad Mother had a headache and went back to my place." He lifted his glass, "To being alone."

"Jenny should be home from her date with Jacob soon." I rested my head on his chest. "Tell me what it was like growing up. Your sister said your mother was different back then."

He kissed the top of my head. "She was. She used to be all soft round edges, and now she's so brittle. Before my father died, she was fun and adventurous. She made up games for my sister and me to play." He took a sip. "My father was the glue that held the family together. I became a reporter because of him. I always thought it was a noble profession. Shining a light into darkness and all that."

"He sounds like he was a good man."

"He was. I was away at school when he died. I kept thinking that I should have been there. That there might have been something I could have done. When they came to tell my mother, she was all alone. My sister and I were both a plane ride away. We came home as fast as we could, but she was somehow resentful that we weren't there when it happened. It's taken me quite a while to process all the bitterness and to realize that none of it was my fault. When I graduated from school, I took an overseas job. I think it was because I couldn't bear to see the blame written on my mother's face. This past week or so has been the longest time we've been together since he died."

"That's so sad." I stroked his face. "You don't regret your career choices, do you?"

He stared at his glass. "No. I think if I regret anything, it's that I somehow failed my mother. Maybe if I had pushed harder, she would have gotten the help she needed. And maybe she'd be happier today."

"That's a lot of ifs. You were scarcely older than Jenny then. Do you think Jenny should be responsible for what happens in my life?"

"Of course not."

"We all chart our own courses. Your father's death must have been a terrible blow for her. But it was horrible for you and your sister too. It doesn't sound like she helped you with your grieving."

"At least my sister and I had each other. When we were younger, we weren't that close because Elizabeth was four years older than me. My father's tragedy erased the age difference, and we banded together. That may have made my mother feel even more isolated." He stood and poured a touch more Bailey's into his glass. He held up the bottle.

"Nope. I'm good."

Rob sat. "I try to focus on the good times we had when we were kids, and how much she loved us then. She probably still loves us; it's just more complicated now. I'm not sure how well I know her anymore."

I kissed him. "You turned out pretty terrific. I love the man you are today."

"Even with my mother?" He pulled me onto his lap.

"Mother and all."

CHAPTER 7

Sunday morning came way too early. My one open eye stole a glance at the clock. *Still time to sleep*. I snuggled back under the covers. Carefully shifting my feet so they wouldn't inadvertently wake one of my sleeping companions, I realized the cats were no longer on the bed. Birds chirped loudly, sounding as if they sat on my windowsill. I yawned. *May as well get up*. I donned sweats and a t-shirt and made my way downstairs.

The cats were on the window seat in the kitchen, their noses pressed against the glass. They seemed entranced by the cardinal hopping back and forth on the cherry tree branch outside the window. An ear twitched as I poured food in their bowls. Courvoisier tore herself away from the riveting view, hopped down, and trotted to her bowl. I chuckled and pushed the start button for coffee.

I laced my sneakers, filled the mug, and pushed the back door open. The cats tripped over each other, trying to beat me out. A dandelion's cheery face mocked me at the edge of the garden. I pulled it and deposited it into my weed bucket. Two more caught my attention. I ripped out the culprits and heard, "You're up early." Alex leaned over the fence. "May I come in?"

"Of course. But don't let the cats out."

I motioned to the Adirondack chairs. "I'm surprised to see you up so early. When we left Ed and Andy's last night, it looked like you were going to be there a while."

She laughed. "When you get older, you don't need as much sleep. It was a fun party."

"I hope you made some new friends."

"Everyone has been so welcoming. I made the right decision on this town."

I cocked my head. "How did you decide on Hopeful?"

"I was tired of the city. All that hustle and bustle. And so impersonal. I don't think I said more than two words to my next-door neighbors in the three years I lived there." She pulled the slide back on her coffee lid and drank.

"That's too bad. Did you grow up in a small town?"

"The smallest. We weren't too far from a city, but our town couldn't have been more than five hundred people on a good day. Then the auto plant closed and our town went into a death spiral. It was time to pull up roots and plant them somewhere else."

"You sound like a true gardener."

"I try." She pointed to the clusters of tulips that were tantalizing us with peeks at their colors. "I also like being able to throw open my back door, set up an easel, and start painting. People pay attention to their gardens here. It gives me such a wonderful place to work."

"I agree. I'm puzzled though. Hopeful isn't that well known. I'm happy you found your way to us, but I'm still not clear how you heard about the town."

"A friend mentioned it. I researched it on the internet, and it looked like a place I'd want to live. And now, my dear, the light is calling me." She picked up her coffee mug and left.

Courvoisier leaped onto my lap and head-butted my hand. I pulled her close. "That sounded logical." I threw the rest of my coffee into the garden and went back inside.

Rob had texted. "Ten thirty Mass okay?"

I checked the clock. "Okay. I'll meet you there." I jumped in the shower, donned better clothing, and ran out the door. Rob and his mother were waiting for me on the steps of the church. "You didn't need to wait outside."

Rob grinned. "Waiting for you gave us a good excuse to enjoy this beautiful day." He extended his arm. "Shall we?" We strolled into the church, Wanda a few steps behind.

I found a relatively empty pew halfway up the aisle. "This work?" I slid in, and Rob and his mother followed me.

After the Mass, Wanda led the way. There was a small cluster of people surrounding Father Tom. He waved us over. I called to Wanda, "Hold up a minute."

She grimaced but stopped.

Father Tom said, "I'd like you to meet two of our newest parishioners, Diedra and Kevin Green." They were older, potentially eighty, with that kind of hair color that was between gray and white. We shook hands.

The skin around Kevin's sky blue eyes crinkled. "Everyone's been so nice to us since we moved in."

"What part of town did you move to?" Rob asked.

Diedra said, "North on Elm. That pretty gray craftsman."

"It is a lovely house. I'm sure you'll be happy."

Kevin said, "We will be." He held out his arm for his wife. "Nice to meet you." They strolled down the steps.

Rob asked. "Can I talk anyone into a late breakfast?"

I raised my hand. "Me."

"I guess so." Wanda shrugged.

Rob led the way to Delightful Bites. He had French toast, I chose blueberry pancakes, and Wanda opted for the low-fat yogurt and berry parfait.

The food came quickly. Wanda took a bite and then gestured toward us with her spoon. "Those people looked very familiar. I just can't remember where I saw them. This is a strange town. I don't know what it is, but I keep on feeling that I know people. It's ridiculous, but the more I try to remember, the farther away it gets from me. Oh well."

* * *

When I got home, I phoned Father Tom's assistant. "Hi, Belinda. Father Tom introduced us to that nice new couple, The Greens."

"They are sweet, aren't they? I met them last Friday when they registered at the church. And Kevin's eyes. Such a beautiful blue. Too bad he's twenty years too old for me." She paused. "Why are you calling, Merry?"

"I wanted to know if you knew where they were from."

Papers shuffled and crinkled. "It's a good thing I decided to straighten up. I was supposed to be on a picnic with my brother."

My palms began to sweat. I met Belinda's brother after Thanksgiving last year, and it wasn't a pleasant experience.

"Here it is. They moved here from Lancaster. That's strange."

"What is?"

"I remember reading that Lancaster was the top town for retirees. I wonder why they came here."

"Maybe our winters are better."

She cackled. "Merry, you are such a card. Well if there's nothing else, I better get back at it." She hung up.

I doodled on the pad in front of me. Hadn't Kathy said her dad's house was in Lancaster? I pushed my phone around the counter with my pencil, then I grabbed it, and pressed Rob's number. "Howdy, stranger."

"Howdy yourself. What's up? I thought you wanted some downtime."

I bit on the eraser. "I did. I have a quick question. Do you know what town Richard's house was in?"

"He had a few houses."

"I'm looking for the one Kathy was talking about. Her family home."

"I don't remember. Hold on." There was a low murmur. "Lancaster. Why?"

"I'll talk to you about it tomorrow." I hung up the phone.

What were the odds that The Greens would move here at the same time Richard was visiting? I needed to find out more. I picked up the phone again and called the Greens' number. "Mrs. Green? Merry March. We met at church today."

"Were you the short woman with curly red hair?"

"Yes. That's me."

"Your beau was so handsome. Kind of reminded me of Kevin when he was younger. Of course, Kevin's eyes are blue, and your man's eyes are green. Oh, listen to me gabbing away. What were you calling about, my dear?"

"The church fete is next Saturday. I wanted to know if you and Mr. Green would like to accompany us there. It's always fun, and you'll be sure to meet a lot of new people."

"We'd love to go."

"Great! We'll swing by your house on our way to the church. I'm looking forward to getting to know you better." I hung up.

Jenny bounded in the back door laughing. Her hair was windblown, and her left hand was in Jacob's. They came to a halt when they saw me at the counter.

"What have you two been up to?"

"Jacob met me after church, and we went hiking near the quarry. Can we make nachos?"

"Of course. There are some green chilies in the cupboard and a jalapeno or two in the fridge if you want to spice it up. I'll let you two have the kitchen." I retreated to the office to give them some space. I still couldn't believe Jenny was old enough to be dating. Where had the time gone?

I pulled up the spreadsheet showing potential college expenses on my computer and gulped. It wasn't likely my ex-husband Drew would send me any money to help; he was still wanted by the Feds. Plus it was doubtful he'd even make an effort. I shuddered. I really didn't want him to try. He'd get me wrapped up in some scheme of his, and I'd have to unwind it again. It was a good thing that Jenny had excellent grades and was researching scholarships. The phone rang. "What's up, Patty?"

"I was driving back from the store, and I saw the guys who used to work for Richard."

"And?" I drew a tulip on an envelope.

"They were driving very slowly past the new couple's house."

"The Greens?"

"Yes, them."

"I asked Mrs. Green to go to the church fete with us. Are you going?"

"Someone talked me into manning one of the booths." Something rustled as if she were unwrapping something.

"What are you eating?"

"A candy bar. I bought it at the store, and I'm trying to finish it before the kids get home, or they'll want one." A door slammed. "Darn it."

A child's voice broke in. "Did you get one for me?"

"No, honey, but you can have the last bite of mine." Patty came back on the phone. "Gotta go." She hung up.

I sketched the church with daffodils edging its outline. *What's so interesting about the Greens?*

✻ ✻ ✻

Wanda complained all the way to the Greens' house. "I don't see why we have to pick up these strangers. In fact, I don't see why I have to go to this Podunk town's anything."

Rob sighed. "Mother, it's not to benefit the town, it's to benefit the church. And as I've told you before, the Greens are new. They don't know anyone."

She sniffed and looked out the window. Rob rolled to a stop in front of their house. I leaped out. "I'll let them know we're here."

The Greens came out the front door, carrying various containers. Mrs. Green balanced one as she shut the front door. I took it from her. "Let me carry that so you can lock the door."

"Oh, we never lock the door, dear. It doesn't seem neighborly."

"I don't think anyone would think badly of you."

Rob popped the trunk open. I shifted the Tupperware to make room for the Greens' items. As I was placing their containers, I sniffed. "Smells like chocolate."

She smiled. "Brownies. They were always a big moneymaker at the church we used to attend."

"I'm sure they'll be a hot ticket here too. Mr. Green, why don't you sit in the front, and I'll slide into the backseat with Wanda and Mrs. Green."

Mrs. Green put her hand on my arm. "No need to be so formal. Call us Diedra and Kevin."

I slid into the back seat, and it was tight. Wanda tsked. "Good thing we aren't going far."

We drove in silence to the church. The vast expanse of green lawn in front had become a sea of white food tents and merchant stalls. Children's delighted squeals signaled the games and small carnival rides on the right. Andy waved me into the next parking space. Wanda got out of the car, and I followed. "Should I add parking attendant to your resume?"

He gave me the evil eye. "Everyone has to do their part. Ed's organizing the food into the appropriate stalls." He extended his arm and pointed to where Ed was standing, clipboard at the ready. Rob helped me unload the trunk, and we trooped toward the food general.

"Lovely day. What did you bring?" He glanced at his clipboard.

Diedra said, "Brownies and Cherry pie."

"Desserts are at that end, over there." He pointed toward the far stall.

I said, "Handheld savory pies and macaroni salad."

"Does the salad need to be refrigerated?"

"No. Olive oil and garlic."

He smiled. "Sounds yummy." He pointed. "The tent right over there."

"I hope you'll get to enjoy the fete!"

We ambled to the tent. Patty stood inside. She checked our dishes and told us where to put them on the table. She put a price tag in front of both. I said, "I feel kind of guilty not helping out."

"You cooked. I chose this so I wouldn't have to. Enjoy yourself. I'll see you later."

The air smelled of popcorn and foods being deep-fried. We met the Greens as they wandered back up the aisle that ran between the booths. Diedra said, "There are some lovely crafts down that way. Kevin was impressed with the birdhouses."

He nodded. "The craftsmanship is terrific."

We strolled the grounds admiring the lovely handmade items, interspersed with carnival vendor trucks. I introduced the Greens to people as we stopped.

Wanda picked up a small wooden birdhouse. The top was a rich mahogany, and the bottom was a light balsam. Both kinds of wood gleamed. A tiny perch protruded below a perfectly round hole. "I love this Christmas ornament. It would be perfect for Elizabeth. She loves birds."

Rob and Kevin tried their hands at a ring toss game. Although their effort was valiant, neither came away with the prize. Wanda stepped forward. "I'd like to try that." Rob paid the vendor. Three flicks of her wrist and each peg was adorned.

Rob's mouth sagged. "Where did you learn to do that?"

"I have many talents." She gestured to the pink bunny. "That one, please. It's silly, I know. But I get a kick out of it." She tucked the rabbit under her arm and said, "I'm hungry. Hopefully, they'll have something I can eat here." She turned toward the main tent.

Diedra followed. "I'm peckish myself." Her husband trailed her.

Rob's eyes were still round. "I can't believe she nailed all three."

"Me either. Did she play a lot of carnival games?"

"Not to my knowledge. Let's catch up to them."

Everyone made their selections, and we found a picnic table. Rob pulled out the benches, and we helped people get seated. I turned to Diedra. "I'm so pleased you chose to settle in our town. It's an undiscovered gem."

She put her sandwich down. "It wasn't that scientific. We knew we wanted to move, so we did some research. When we told our priest the places we were thinking about, he told us all about Father Tom. We knew that this was the place for us."

"Didn't you used to live in Lancaster?"

Diedra gave me a sharp glance. "Who told you that?"

"Not sure. I remember someone mentioning it." I took a sip of the cola.

Her shoulders relaxed. "Oh. It's not like it's a secret or anything."

"Lancaster's so lovely. I'm surprised you wanted to leave."

Kevin sipped his coffee. "This place is nice too."

Wanda stopped playing with her salad. "It's odd, but you two look very familiar. My husband Richard Franco used to live in Lancaster. Maybe you knew him?"

Diedra dropped her fork. "Your husband? But when you introduced yourself, I thought you said your last name was Jenson."

"It is. I've been married several times, but I haven't changed my name since I married my first husband."

Kevin broke in. "But didn't he just die?"

"No, no. My husband's been dead for twenty years."

Rob cleared his throat. "Mom, I don't think they meant Dad, they meant Richard."

"Oh. Richard. Yes, he did die. Quite unfortunate."

I kept my head down, but a smile threatened. It wasn't funny, but I couldn't believe how cavalier Wanda was about her dead fifth husband. I stood. "Does anyone want dessert, or would you prefer to stroll first?"

Wanda said, "Let's stretch our legs."

There were nods in unison, so Rob helped me clean the table.

I walked out of the tent with Diedra. I pointed toward some of the kiosks we hadn't yet visited. "Shall we start over here?"

She nodded.

"I would find it difficult to leave Hopeful. So many memories with Jenny. Did you get tired of the town?"

"Not at all. We wanted to experience something new."

CHAPTER 8

Rob and I sat in the backyard. There was the slightest nip in the air, and I grabbed a throw from the hope chest near the back door and tucked it around my legs. "Why do you think Diedra and Kevin decided to move? I could think of a lot more exotic places if I were looking for new experiences."

"Scandal? Death? Mean people?"

I swirled the wine in my glass. "Mean people might be a stretch."

"I'll do some research tomorrow and see what I can find out."

"Thanks." I pulled Rob's hand to my lips and kissed it. "What do you think your mother has been up to?"

"What do you mean?"

"She borrowed my car before Richard died and disappeared for an entire day. And now she has yours."

"Do you want me to tell her to rent a car?"

I pushed his shoulder. "Don't be silly. It seems odd. Does she have friends here we don't know about?"

"Now that you mention it, it is strange. I'll ask her. But I don't know that I'll get a lot out of her. As you have no doubt guessed, she's a very private person."

The light from Ed and Andy's back deck turned on. Andy appeared in the doorway and waved. "Can we join you?"

"If you have folding chairs. Mine are still in storage."

He held up his finger and disappeared under the deck. A flashlight wobbled. He came back out and directed the flashlight on two chairs. "Success."

Ed walked out onto the deck, carrying a container and a supermarket bag. Andy waited for him, and they strolled across the alley and into my backyard. Rob retrieved two more glasses, as Andy unfolded the chairs.

Ed plopped the bag on the table. "Cheesecake I didn't take to the church fete. Anyone interested? It's topped with cherries."

I held up my hand. "Talked me into it."

"Me too." Rob poured wine into the glasses.

Ed handed us pieces and picked up his wine glass. He toasted, "To a successful day."

I raised my glass, "To two hard workers, the church is lucky to have."

Andy said, "I'll drink to that."

I put a bite of cheesecake in my mouth. "I'm going to need the recipe."

The outside light went on next door. Alex called, "Is it a party? Can anyone join?"

I answered, "Yes to both questions. All you need is a lawn chair."

She bundled through the gate, chair in hand. Rob produced another glass. Ed asked, "Cheesecake?"

She unfolded the chair, saying, "Of course. Isn't it lovely tonight? No bugs yet and the faintest hint of chill still in the air. Won't find me out here in late June."

I raised my glass, "To impromptu parties."

We drank. Alex lifted the plate to her nose and sniffed. "No nuts, right? Just want to be careful."

Ed smiled. "Smart to double-check. Just normal cheesecake ingredients and cherries."

She took a bite. "Yum. I probably could have tree nuts, but I don't want to chance it."

"We missed you at the church fete today." I placed my glass on the arm of the chair.

"I had a show already scheduled that I couldn't get out of. I would have much preferred to support the church by showing my art there."

"Ed and Andy did their usual great job moving people and their offerings to where they needed to be."

Andy raised his glass to me. "I had one of your meat pies. It was terrific."

Rob topped off the glasses. "Alex, where did you live before here?"

"Oh, you know, here and there." She tucked her foot underneath her.

Ed said, "Alex once lived in San Diego. She used to surf."

My eyes widened. "I've never met a surfer before. Was it hard to learn?"

"Patience is the key. You have to wait for the exact moment to strike. Many people are too eager, want immediate gratification. They don't succeed. Its people like me, those who are willing hunker down, lie in wait, who get the best and longest rides." She examined her glass.

"Sounds like a life lesson more than just surfing."

Her blue eyes met mine. "I think so."

* * *

Drambuie stood on my chest, batting at my face. "What? It isn't that late." The clock rang nine. "Oops. I guess it is. Sorry." I pulled on pants and a t-shirt and strolled down the stairs, yawning the whole way. I stabbed the coffee button with my finger. "Hurry up."

The cats continued weaving about my legs. I pulled out their food and scooped some into a bowl. "Here. Let it be noted that you are fed before I've had my first coffee." Unconcerned, they abandoned their dance, and within seconds, both faces were head down in their bowls.

I poured the coffee and sighed as I had my first sip. I wandered toward the bay window and parted the curtains. Alex gathered her art supplies. She folded the easel and ducked back into the house. I guess the early morning light was gone.

I let go of the curtain, and it swung back into place. There was a swift knock at the door, and Rob walked in carrying donuts. I took the bag. "Heaven. Is there an old fashioned plain in here?"

He stepped back, hand to his heart. "Would I dare come in without one?"

"Then you may have coffee." I gestured toward the pot.

He retrieved a mug and poured. "I have to get back to my place in a few minutes. I told Mother that I was going for a walk."

My right eyebrow lifted.

"I needed some space. I tried asking her what she'd been up to lately, and she got offended. She told me that she was over seventy, and she didn't have to account for her time to a son who's slightly north of forty."

"Oh my."

"Yes. I told you asking questions never goes well with her." He sat at the table, dug out a cruller, and took a bite.

"Maybe I should try it. Is she going to church with us today?"

"Yes."

"I'll take her to lunch afterward. Maybe she'll be in a good mood and talk."

He put the last of the donut in his mouth and kissed my cheek. "I love your optimism. See you at ten-thirty."

I broke off a piece of the plain donut and tossed it in my mouth. The clock rang ten. I leaped up. A quick shower, some hurried dressing, and I was out the door.

After church, Wanda and I strolled to the Golden Skillet. The hostess led us to a booth toward the rear of the restaurant. I slid in so that the back of my head faced the door. On a busy Sunday, I hoped there'd be fewer interruptions if people didn't see me.

We ordered, and the food was delivered quickly. Wanda got her usual yogurt parfait, and I opted for the banana French toast. I bathed it in butter and syrup. Wanda gasped, "Merry, dear if you continue to eat like that, you'll be as big as a house."

I cut a piece. The aroma of warm bananas and vanilla made my mouth water. I took a bite. "It's wonderful. Would you like some?"

Her lips pursed. She shook her head and bent toward her yogurt.

"Thanks for coming with me. I thought it would be good to have some time to chat."

She stirred her parfait, blending the fruit, yogurt, and nuts. Her eyes lifted to mine. "Chat?"

"Yes. You've been in town for a few weeks. Have you made any new friends?"

She put the spoon down. "My husband died, and I've been charged with his murder. It's hardly the time for me to be making friends."

I slid the whipped cream topping off my plate and onto a smaller dish. There was such a thing as gilding the lily. "Of course. I just wondered what you've found to do. It seems like you're filling your days."

She pushed the parfait away. "What I do is my business." She stood. "Thank you for brunch." She stalked out the door.

I sighed, cut another piece of French toast, and swirled it in the syrup pooling on the plate.

* * *

"I told you she was sensitive." Rob passed me a dish to put away.

"But where has she been? We still don't know."

"She asked to borrow my car again at three." He bent to pull the silverware holder from the dishwasher, placing it on the counter.

"Should we follow her?"

He sorted the silverware into the drawer. "Yep. But there'll be hell to pay if she catches us."

I slid the glasses into the cupboard. "But then at least we'd know."

"Better get going." He picked up his phone.

We drove to his house, gliding to a stop two houses down from his. He said, "Kind of reminds me of the time we trailed Paula Sanders."

"Let's hope it works out better than when Patty and I trailed those two guys who worked for Richard."

"That's not funny. I hate when you put yourself at risk." He pointed toward his house, where his car backed out of the garage. "And here we go."

I waited until she had turned on to the main street to follow. Two cars went by after her, and then I pulled out. She paused at the stoplight to turn left. Luckily another car sat behind her. I pulled into the turn lane, and the light changed. She and the car in front went, and then the green arrow disappeared. Oncoming traffic ensued, and five cars went by before I was able to turn. I sped up.

Rob pointed toward a car in the distance. "I think that's her. Good thing she's stuck behind that big piece of planting equipment." We joined the line of cars waiting to pass the slow-moving piece of farm machinery. "Her turn signal is on. I think she's going to get on the highway." She turned onto the entrance ramp. A few other cars followed, and then I was able to make the same turn.

She stayed in the right-hand lane. I said, "It doesn't look like she's going to stay on long." The sign for the next exit appeared, and her turn signal flashed. "I guess we're getting off here." I made the turn. She waited at the stop sign and then turned right. "It looks like she knows where she is going."

I crept along behind her. A sign for an animal shelter appeared, and she turned into the parking lot. It was a squat building, with a large gray door in the center. The dark brown exterior had cute yellow cat and dog paw prints decorating the front.

Pulling in behind her, I parked on the other side of the lot. She primped for a few minutes and then left the car. It beeped as she locked it. "Looks like it's going to be a while." I turned off the car. "Is your mother an animal lover? I don't think she's ever petted my cats, and they are pretty cute."

"She's never been big on animals. My sister begged for a dog, but she never allowed us to get a pet. Not even a hamster."

"Should we go in? We could pretend to be looking for a new furball."

"The place doesn't look that big. She's sure to see us."

The side door opened. An older gentleman in a white coat exited, arm-in-arm, with Rob's mother. She was smiling at him.

My mouth dropped. "Is this number six? And it looks like he's a vet. I hope she's changed her mind about animals."

They climbed into what looked like a brand new gunmetal gray Mercedes roadster. Wanda pulled a scarf from her purse and secured her hair. Rob's eyes widened, "I don't know if I've ever seen Mother in a convertible before."

"Should I follow?"

"Please do."

I let them exit the lot and waited for a few cars. Then I made a sharp turn back onto the road. We wound around the curving tree-lined boulevard until the Mercedes made a right hand turn onto a cobblestone drive. The car paused as ornate black steel gates swung inward. I passed the driveway and pulled over a few hundred feet ahead. The house was on a hill in the distance, about an acre distant. It looked like one of those expensive Tudors you'd find on the Main Line in Philadelphia, but a lot larger. Massive timbers highlighted the front elevation and included a lovely arch that the Mercedes passed through moving toward where I assumed the garages would be.

I waited for a moment and then made a U-turn. I passed the drive again, but more slowly. Rob took a picture of the house number welded into the gate and then used Google Maps to find out what street we were on. I continued to drive. When I spied a coffee shop in the distance, I pointed. "Let's stop there."

Rob's face had a pinched look. "Okay."

I put the car in park. "What do you think that's all about?"

He got out of the car. "It looks like Mother has found her next ex." He shook his head, frowning. "One would think that she'd wait for Richard's body to be colder before she moved on. Plus, with all the money she's getting, I thought she might swear off men for a while."

We ordered two coffees. I handed one to Rob. "What's next?"

"I'm going to find out who this guy is. His house looks far too fancy for a country veterinarian."

* * *

I started dinner while Rob set the table. The cats watched me wash the chicken, ever hopeful. His phone dinged. He held it out to me. It was from his mom: "Dinner out tonight. Back by eleven."

"I guess I need one less plate." He put the extra back in the cupboard.

I basted the chicken thighs with a honey-soy glaze and slid the pan into the oven. "We have about forty-five minutes. What did you find out about your mother's new friend?"

"I need a glass of wine. Would you like one?" I retrieved two wine glasses.

We sat next to each other on the sofa, and Rob put his arm around me. "It turns out the guy was a Wall Street trader who was a wunderkind. He made a boatload of cash and then hung it up when he turned fifty. Apparently, his dream was always to work with animals. So he enrolled in veterinary school at fifty-five. He owns the place we saw. He employs several other vets and technicians, and his clients give him five-star ratings."

"It's nice that he loves animals. Maybe he's a nice guy."

His fingers tightened on the wine glass. "I don't care if he's Gandhi. She should have waited. At least another month or so." He put the glass down. "Sorry. I don't mean to be such a downer, but she's under suspicion of murder. How will the police feel when they find out she has another one on a string?" He rubbed the back of his neck. "Or even worse, if they find out she was seeing him before Richard died. She's a pain, but she's my mother. I don't want her to go to jail."

I put my arm around his waist and pulled him close. "How are the police going to find out about it? He lives a half-hour away. And she's not going to tell anyone; she hasn't even told you."

He kissed my forehead. "You're right. I'm probably worrying over nothing."

"I need to get the rice going. Do you want to put together a salad?"

"You got it."

Jenny pounded down the stairs. "When's dinner?"

"Twenty minutes."

She sat at the table. "Is there anything I can do?"

"We've got it."

She scrolled on her phone. "Huh."

I stirred the rice and covered it. "Huh, what?"

"It's strange, that's all."

"Jenny, stop being so cryptic. What's strange?"

She walked over to the stove. "Look."

"What am I looking at?"

"Jacob's dad and mom went to some charity thing tonight to benefit animal shelters in the area." She put the phone in my hand. "Here. Doesn't that look like Mr. Jenson's mom? And who's the guy she's clinging to?"

Wanda's face was tipped toward her new beau; her expression was like the one Nancy Reagan wore when she looked at Ronnie.

Rob took the phone from me and enlarged the picture. "Yep. That's Mom. And the vet. Hopefully, no one from the police will see this."

Jenny took back her phone. She scrolled through a few more photos and handed it back. A picture of Jay and his wife Barbara stared back at us. I gulped.

CHAPTER 9

I *hate Mondays.* I scrolled through my calendar. Busy day. I gave my eyelashes a few licks of mascara and walked out the door.

The redbuds were blooming, and the lilacs didn't look like they'd be far behind. My breathing slowed, and I began to enjoy the walk. The woman at the end of the block had cut back her ornamental grasses and set wireframes on top of the peonies. They looked close enough to burst through in the next week or so. I made a mental note to get my frames out before it was too late.

I walked into my office when Rob texted: "Lunch at my place with Mother?"

"Fine. But I only have an hour."

I pushed through the door. People were hunched over their phones, beginning the day's work. Cheryl followed me into my office. "I have news."

My eyebrow rose as I put my purse in a drawer. "Yes?"

"My sister-in-law called. Your eventual mother-in-law is the talk of the police station."

I sat and extended my hand to the seat opposite. "Why?"

"They said that Wanda attended the 'Dollars Mean Happy Pets' fundraiser last night." She sank onto the chair and leaned closer to the desk. "She was there with someone."

"I saw the pictures. Their photographer must have been a busy beaver because she posted them as the party was going on. Don't they usually do some editing? What if they got a donor's bad side?"

Her face fell. "You already knew?"

"I knew that she was there, but I didn't know that Wanda was the talk of the station."

"They're saying this gives her an additional motive."

I rubbed my forehead. "I'm sure she just met him."

"From what I heard, they were very cozy for people who barely know each other." Cheryl stood. "Here's your call list today. Oh, and the Humphries will be by at ten to talk about moving to an auto plan that charges by the mile."

I took the list. "Got it. I need to leave by noon to go to Rob's place. I should be back before my one o'clock appointment, but I'll let you know if I'm delayed."

She shut the door behind her. I banged my head lightly on the desk. *Love family.* I picked up the phone and got on with my day.

Before noon, I trudged out the door, dreading the conversation we were about to have. *Put on your big girl pants.* I sped up and knocked briefly at Rob's front door before heading in.

Wanda sat at Rob's dining room table. Her eyebrows arched. "I didn't know you were joining us for lunch. What a pleasant surprise."

Rob came out of the kitchen carrying a platter of sandwiches. "Thanks for coming." He gave me a quick peck on the cheek and put down the platter. "I got an assortment of sandwiches, so you can choose the one you want."

Wanda stood. "It's such a lovely day. I'm going to have iced tea. Anyone else want one?"

I raised my finger; Rob did the same. Wanda strolled into the kitchen. I whispered, "What's the plan?"

"No plan. I'm going to tell her we know."

I leaned closer to him. "She was the talk of the station this morning."

I jumped as Wanda came back into the room with a pitcher of iced tea. "What's all the whispering about? You two look as guilty as kids who took the last piece of chocolate."

Rob took the pitcher from her and poured three glasses. "It's about last night."

I stuffed a potato chip in my mouth and stared at my lap.

Wanda selected a half sandwich and set it down on her plate. "What about last night?"

"We saw pictures of you online with a new man. And he didn't look like a recent acquaintance."

I retrieved another chip from the bag and ate it.

Wanda's gaze fixed on me. "Stop that. Take a sandwich and eat real food." She passed me the platter.

I slid an egg salad onto my plate, shook a few chips out to join it, and then passed the platter to Rob. Wanda took a bite of her turkey sandwich.

Rob stared at his mother. "Aren't you going to say anything?"

"I hate the internet."

He put half a roast beef hoagie on his plate. "That wasn't the kind of conversation I thought we might have."

"It's intrusive." She dabbed her lips with a napkin. "What do you want me to say? I have a new friend, yes. He's very nice."

I placed my sandwich back on my plate. "If you don't mind me asking, how long have you known the gentleman?"

She glared at me. "Not that it's any of your business, but we met a few months ago when Richard and I were in the Bahamas. Mac was there for a refresher course on some type of dog disorder. Richard had gone to bed early, and Mac and I found ourselves next to each other at the blackjack table."

Rob's mouth dropped. "You play blackjack?"

Wanda smiled. "You must think I've led a very sheltered life. I like to try new things. A well-rounded person is more appealing."

"You sound like you're a product to be bought."

Her head tilted. "Not bought, dear. That's so vulgar. I prefer to think of myself as someone who can be appreciated."

I interjected, "Let's get back to the matter at hand, shall we?"

"Yes. Mother, don't you realize how bad this looks?" Rob gulped the tea.

"What on earth do you mean?"

"The money Richard left is a great motive for killing him. Now the police have another. A new man. They could say that you wanted to leave Richard. Did Richard have you sign a prenup before you married him?"

"Of course. We both signed one. I wanted to protect my assets too."

Rob put his head in his hands.

I said, "Don't you see? Richard's dying means you inherit the money and are free for the new man."

Wanda sat back in her chair. "I hadn't thought of it like that."

* * *

I craved a latte the next morning, so I swung by Delightful Bites. Diedra was in line. As she got her coffee, she walked past me. I waved, "Good morning. In the mood for coffee too?"

"Oh, hello, Merry. She held up her cup. "It's so good here. I keep thinking that I should make do with what we have at home, but today I decide to live a little."

The line shifted forward, and I kept pace. "Do you have a few minutes?" I motioned toward the tables. "We could sit here."

"I do." She moved to a café table with a view of the street.

I purchased a latte and a luscious looking raspberry-filled French braid pastry. At the coffee station, I took a packet of sugar and two forks. I set the pastry on the table between us. "I'm hoping you're going to share this with me."

"This is my lucky day. Raspberry is my favorite." She picked up one of the forks and took a bite. "Delicious. The pastry is so flaky and buttery."

I poured half a packet of sugar into my coffee and stirred. "I much prefer my coffee in a real cup."

She lifted her paper cup. "Either way it's good coffee. Thanks again for taking us to the church event. It was fun."

"I can't believe Rob's mother kept the bunny she won. I thought for sure she would have given it to one of the kids there."

"I think she wanted to bask in her win." She gave me a half-smile. "After all, the boys didn't do very well."

"Do you and your husband have children?"

"Oh, yes. We have five. And ten grandchildren. They are the light of my life."

"Five kids. Sometimes I have difficulty managing one."

She stirred her coffee. "They had their moments to be sure, but I wouldn't have traded one of them." Her voice cracked. "Not a one. Our oldest daughter died a few years back. It was like losing part of myself." She slid her cup away. "I don't think I'll ever get over it."

I touched her arm. "I'm so sorry for your loss."

"It's the reason we moved. Too many memories."

"She must have been so young."

"Only thirty. She and her husband left our house to drive home. There was a curve. They didn't make it." Diedra looked me in the eye. "They weren't drinking, although the police suspected they were at first. They found that they were going a bit fast. Forty-five in a thirty-five mile an hour zone. But the real problem was their brake lines. They'd been cut, and no one was charged." A tear escaped and trickled down her cheek.

✳ ✳ ✳

Rob stopped by the office after work. "Want to go out?"

"Where's your mom?"

He sighed. "She was with the police again, answering more questions. Tonight, she's with the new beau. She wants me to meet him this weekend."

I kissed his cheek. "Hopefully he's nicer than the last one." I pulled my purse from my desk. "Jenny's at the Twilligers' tonight. Where do you want to go?"

"Fiorella's?"

I hopped into his car. He turned on a jazz station for the short drive.

I slid into the booth, and we ordered. "I have news." I filled him in on my conversation with Diedra.

"So you think that Richard ordered a hit on them?"

"The story matched the one Kathy told me. I googled the story. Diedra's daughter's married name was Peabody."

"Same story and same name." He sipped his wine.

"Plus their brakes were cut. And they lived in Lancaster. Same town. Gotta be the same people."

"I agree." Our food arrived, and I pushed my stuffed shells around the plate. "It's so sad to think of their lives being cut short. And by someone we knew."

"Let's get this to go. You don't look like you're making much headway, and maybe we'll be more in the mood to eat later." He motioned for the waiter, who took our plates back to the kitchen and returned with a large bag.

I put the bag in the oven on low heat when we returned to my house and held up another container. "They gave us three cannolis."

He unscrewed the cork from a wine bottle. "That was nice of them."

"It was."

The smell of garlic and tomato sauce filled the room. My stomach growled. "I guess I am hungry, after all." I took the food from the oven and put it on the table. "Let's eat."

Rob speared a sausage. "I got a call from Mother's lawyer. The police want to talk to her again."

"That can't be good."

"It makes me nervous."

* * *

Patty texted Thursday night: "Are you home alone?"

"Yes. Out back." The sun was on the wane, and a warm breeze caressed my face.

A few minutes later, Patty unhooked the gate and rushed into the backyard. "Kids are in bed, Patrick's watching sports, and I have news."

I waved toward the house. "Get a glass of wine. And one for me too, while you're up."

She scampered up the steps and returned with two extremely full glasses of wine. I raised one eyebrow. She handed me a drink. "So I don't have to bring out the bottle."

I smirked. "Sound plan."

She sat at the edge of her chair. "I got a job."

I set my glass down. "That's great. Where?"

"I'm going to design the new Shades of Gray store."

"So Caroline finally sold it." I kicked some dirt off the paver by my feet. Caroline's sister, Amanda, had been killed last year, and Caroline had inherited the building.

"She'd been talking to Amanda's assistant, but that fell through. Two sisters bought it. April and Sandy Poole. Caroline remembered that I had been doing some initial design work for the assistant, so she recommended they look me up. They liked my initial plans and hired me." A grin split her face. "We're going to the happy hour on Friday at the Pickled Herring. I would appreciate it if you and Rob would show up to town."

I raised my glass. "To the best interior designer in town."

She touched her glass to mine. "Thank you kindly. But that's not all my news."

I raised my left eyebrow. "There's more?"

She pushed my shoulder. "You have to keep this under your hat, but Patrick took one of those DNA tests—you know—the ones that show where your ancestors came from. He was torn. He loves his adoptive parents so much; you've met them. They're sweet. He was afraid it'd upset them. They urged him to do it, but it was only when I pointed out that our kids should know where they came from that he agreed. So I got a kit for his birthday last month."

"Did he send it in?"

"He did. And he just got the breakdown back. His ancestors were from Northern Europe. The biggest percentages were from Ireland-England, and the next highest were from Germany-France." She paused to take a breath. "Isn't it cool?"

"It is." I studied the wine in my glass. "So did he discover any long lost relatives?"

She took a sip. "He hasn't logged in yet. He has to opt-in to be able to find his relatives." She leaned back in the chair. "Of course, any relatives would have to do the same. I don't want to get his hopes up, but I wish he would go online to see what they have."

"I guess you're going to have to give him some time to get comfortable with this."

She sighed. "I suppose so. Well, that's all my news. What's been going on in your life?"

"Let me see if I can sum it up for you. Wanda has a very public new beau who's a veterinarian she started dating before the demise of her

husband, and not surprisingly the police want to talk with her again."
I sipped my wine. "Oh, yes. And the Greens?"

She nodded.

"They moved to Hopeful from Lancaster, where Richard lived, and
where Richard had their eldest daughter and her husband killed."

Her mouth dropped. "That's terrible. What a horrible man. How's
Rob handling all this?"

"Every time he turns around, his mother throws another surprise
at him. I think he doesn't know what to believe anymore. He's starting
to feel like a top that never stops spinning."

"What do you think?"

"We're accumulating suspects."

She stood. "In my experience, people who love animals are
generally good souls. And now, I need to return home." I kissed her
cheek, took her empty wine glass, and made my way back into the
house.

I put her glass in the dishwasher. About to dump the rest of my
wine in the sink, I hesitated and then downed it. Nothing like a little
pick me up during the workweek. I flipped the deadbolt and toddled
up to bed.

CHAPTER 10

It was after five when Rob and I walked into the Pickled Herring. Patty waved to us from the far side of the bar. "Over here."

We made our way to where she was standing. I said, "It's crowded in here tonight."

Patty nodded. She held her hand toward the two striking strawberry blondes on her left. "This is April and her sister, Sandy."

I shook their hands. "It's nice to meet you." They looked to be in their late thirties and were a tad overdressed for the local pub. Their clothes were beautiful. April wore a lovely form-fitting coral dress with a white jacket, and Sandy wore a cobalt blue dress with a tricolored sash around her narrow waist. "I love your clothes."

April laughed. "It's a bit much for the venue—" her hand encompassed the bar "—but, it's good advertising for the shop."

Sandy chimed in, "Everyone is so welcoming. We can't wait to show people our clothes."

"When is the Grand Opening?" Rob handed me a glass of wine.

April turned to Patty. "It depends on when our designer will be done."

"One month, maybe sooner." Patty raised her glass.

"One month," we echoed back, as we lifted our drinks.

Patrick wandered in from outside. He kissed Patty on her cheek and signaled to Ann for a beer. She put it on the bar by his elbow. I made my way to his side. "Exciting stuff!"

"Yeah. It's great that Patty got this job."

"I was talking about the DNA test."

He swigged his beer. "I'm still not sure how I feel about it."

"Don't you want to know if you have long lost relatives?"

"What if I find out they're all like Rob's mother?"

Rob sidled up and poked him in the ribs. "Hey. Enough about my mother."

"Sorry." He gave Rob a rueful grin.

"Why are we talking about mothers?"

Patty, April, and Sandy moved closer to the bar. Patrick said, "I took a DNA test. I have to go to their website and opt-in if I want to see my relations." He laughed. "What are the chances a relative did the DNA test and opted-in? I don't know why I'm so worried."

April said, "They have free wifi here, and you have a smartphone, right?"

Ann wiped the bar nearby. She pointed to Patrick's phone. "The password's frenchfry."

Patty pulled Patrick's face close to hers. "You don't have to do this."

He shook his head. "There's probably nothing to it. I don't know why I'm dilly-dallying." He picked up his phone, tapped in the website address, and logged in. "Okay, I'm checking the box to opt for more information." His finger hovered over the box.

The gathered crowd shouted, "Do it!"

And he dramatically clicked. A second later, he pulled the phone to him, blocking our view. His grip tightened, and he paled.

Patty grabbed his arm. "What is it?"

His gaze met hers. "I have a brother." He sank onto the bar stool. "I have a half-brother. He's younger than me, and he lives in Idaho."

❋ ❋ ❋

I tipped the pizza delivery guy and brought the box to the kitchen. Rob took it from me and placed it on the trivet in the middle of the table. "What were the chances of that happening?"

"Patrick finding out that he had a brother?" I opened the box and slid a slice of cheese on my plate.

Rob pointed to one with sausage. "Yes. And for him to find out about it in a bar. It must have been tough to have all of us staring at him when he found out."

"We're all friends." I leveraged a spatula under the piece he wanted and deposited it on his plate.

He sprinkled Italian seasoning. "Not all of us. There were new people there."

"April and Sandy?"

His mouth was full, so he nodded.

"Okay, then new friends."

Jenny bounded in the back door. "Ooh. Pizza."

"I thought you had dinner out."

"We ate early, and I'm still hungry." She retrieved a plate from the cupboard, waltzed over, and took a piece with sausage.

Rob said, "Hey. Those are mine."

"You weren't going to eat them all. Besides, sausage is fattening." She took a large bite.

"You're starting to sound like my mother." He slid another piece on his plate.

I turned to Jenny. "What did you do after dinner?"

"Talked to Dad."

My mouth dropped. "How did you talk to him?"

"On Jacob's PC."

"You do know your father's a fugitive? You could get into trouble." I pushed my half-eaten slice away. "You could get Jacob into trouble."

"That's why we went to his house. Jacob's IP address bounces all over the world. There's no way they could trace it." She lifted another slice from the box. "He doesn't do anything bad with it; he's a part-time hacker."

"I'm not sure that being a hacker, either full- or part-time, is a good thing."

She looked down her nose at me. "Anyway, Dad and Arianna love Brunei. He said the seafood is yummy. And he got a job. He's working for one of the money management firms investing for expats."

My ex-husband Drew was a swindler of the highest magnitude. He and his fashion-model girlfriend moved to Brunei just ahead of the Feds arresting them. They chose Brunei because it didn't have an extradition treaty with the United States. I groaned. "Why on earth would they hire him to handle money with his history?"

"I'm going to assume he didn't tell them, and they don't have access to U.S. databases." Rob pushed his plate away.

I turned to Jenny. "You need to promise me something."

She paused, slice mid-way to her lips. "What?"

"You can't help your dad. And you can't take money from him."

Her eyes widened, and she put the slice down. "What about school. How are we going to afford college?"

"We'll manage. You don't need to worry. You need to keep your grades as good as they are and your hands clean. I don't want him to ruin your future. And I don't want to have to clean up after him again."

"I guess. But what if he needs me? He's still my dad."

Rob leaned forward. "He is. But he's also an adult. If he's going to get into trouble, you don't want to be any part of it."

I stood. "Unless I need to say anything further on the subject—" Jenny shook her head. "Who wants homemade oatmeal raisin cookies?"

She gave a half-hearted wave. "Milk too, please."

✳ ✳ ✳

Rob texted first thing Saturday morning: "Brunch with my mother and new beau? Please? Golden Skillet, ten-thirty."

"Meet you there."

I examined the thermometer. Still chilly. I opted for gray slacks, a green shirt, and a white cardigan. Wardrobe set, I hopped into the shower.

Jenny knocked on the bathroom door as I toweled my hair dry. I opened it. "What's up?"

She sat on the closed toilet seat. "Do you think Jacob could get in trouble for helping me contact Dad?"

I sighed as I leaned against the counter. "I don't know. If he's the tech wizard you think he is, maybe not."

"But there's a chance?"

"There's always a chance."

"Then I won't ask him to do it again. I don't want him to get into trouble for me."

I walked over and lifted her chin. "That's probably a wise decision."

She frowned. "I miss him."

"I know honey. Sometimes the decisions others make have real repercussions for the people they love." My head tilted. "If he turned himself in, at least you could visit him in prison."

"That's not funny."

"I didn't mean it to be. My number one job is making sure you stay out of trouble. And if that means you aren't able to have contact with your dad, so be it."

Her eyes brimmed with tears. "That's mean."

I knelt next to her. "Jenny, this is important. Your dad made bad choices in his life, and unfortunately, it looks like he's still making them. You're so young, and you have your whole life ahead of you. Don't screw it up. I know your dad wouldn't want anything bad to happen to you."

Tears dripped from her face. "So what you're saying I can't talk to him? That Dad is out of my life? Who's going to walk me down the aisle when I get married?"

I hugged her. "Who knows what might happen in the future. Maybe this whole mess will go away. Let's worry about today, and let tomorrow take care of itself." I handed her a tissue. "I love you."

She stood. "I love you too. But this sucks." She stomped from the room.

I reached for mascara. *She's right. It stinks, but it's Drew's fault.* The clock downstairs chimed ten. I finished donning minimal makeup, grabbed my purse, and headed out the door.

The crabapples were starting to bloom, and the magnolias were close to spent. It looked like the lilac flowers would soon open. I loved their spicy-sweet scent. My pace slowed. I stopped to talk to one of my clients. Her garden was amazing. My phone buzzed, and I jumped. "I'm late. See you later."

Rob's text read: "Where are you?"

"Almost there." I turned left into town and stepped up my pace. Rob, Wanda, and Mac stood on the sidewalk outside the restaurant. I hurried to meet them. "I'm sorry. I was talking to one of my clients, and time got away from me. You could have gone inside."

Rob said, "Merry, this is Glen MacNamara."

He extended his hand. "Everyone calls me Mac."

"It's lovely to meet you. Shall we go in?"

Wanda gave a terse nod, we moved into the restaurant, and were seated. They gave us my favorite booth. I loved looking at the cow collection that rimmed the window. I touched the nearest one for luck and turned my attention to Mac. "I understand you're a veterinarian."

"I had enough of Wall Street and decided to return to my childhood dream. I grew up on a farm and idolized the vet who came to take care of the animals. He was so competent. He never seemed surprised, handled whatever nature threw at him. I remember one time there was this cow about to give birth—"

Wanda cleared her throat.

He laughed. "That's what I like about this woman. She always lets me know when I'm going too far." He took her hand. "I can't tell you how great it is to have found a woman who cares as much about animals as I do."

Rob's eyes widened.

I kicked his foot. "Wanda mentioned that you met at a casino."

"Well, I can't lie. I'm no stranger to the tables. My favorite game is blackjack." He kissed Wanda's hand. "That's her favorite too."

Luckily the waitress came with our order. She passed the plates around. Rob stared at his meal.

I cut the egg atop my crab benedict. It oozed, mixing with the hollandaise sauce. "Mac, I'm sorry if we're quiet. This is a lot to take in. After all, Richard's only been dead a few weeks."

"I'm sorry he's dead, but Wanda was going to leave him anyway." He raised her hand to his lips. "Weren't you honey bear?"

Rob made a choking sound. "Honey bear?"

"It's my nickname for her. She's sweet and such a warm person."

Rob stood. "I'm sorry. This is too much. Mother, I'll see you back at my place." He stalked off.

Food congealed on my plate. "I think I should go after him. It was nice meeting you, Mac." I stood and hurried out the door.

Rob was two blocks ahead when I strode out. He looked like he was sprinting. I sighed and stopped at Delightful Bites. I selected a few Danishes and then made my way to Rob's house. When I walked in, he was pacing the living room floor. I set the bag down on the counter.

"Can you believe it? Sitting there, talking about his relationship with my mother like there was nothing wrong. And her! I don't know who that woman is. She likes animals? That's a new one for me. What is wrong with that woman?"

I hugged him. "Calm down. Have a seat, and let's talk about it."

He continued to pace. "Maybe she killed him. It sounds like Mac thought she was going to leave Richard." He stopped and grimaced. "Who am I kidding?" He dropped onto a chair. "She killed him for the money." He rubbed the back of his neck. "My mother is a murderess."

I dropped down next to him. "You don't know that. Sure, she's squirrely, but that doesn't mean she murdered anyone. Maybe Mac killed him. Maybe he saw them go into the hotel room, and he lost it."

"I could believe that if he was shot or beaten, but he was poisoned. That takes premeditation." He gasped. "What if they were in on it together?"

"Why would he kill Richard? He thought your mother was leaving him." I retrieved coffee from the cupboard and measured it into the machine. "It is odd that she decided to have one last fling with Richard. She had to have been seeing Mac while she was here; she kept borrowing the car."

He took a Danish from the bag and tore a piece off. "I feel sick."

I handed him a cup of coffee. "Drink this; you'll feel better." I sat next to him. "Let's not get ahead of ourselves. We don't know if she did it. Don't forget, the Greens have a motive too. We don't even know that the poison was in the champagne. At any rate, I think you need to have a heart-to-heart with your mother."

He popped the piece of Danish into his mouth. "I have a bad feeling about this."

CHAPTER 11

I was dusting the living room furniture when the doorbell rang. Pulling it open, I gasped when I saw Richard's two henchmen. Frank, the one with the scar, said, "Can we come in? We need to talk to you."

"I'll come out. It's too nice a day to be inside." I tossed my dust rag onto the floor and shut the door behind me. We stood awkwardly on the stoop.

Bud backed down onto the step below. "We need to talk."

I shuffled so that my back pressed against the door, trying not to look nervous, but my eyes were skittering between the two men. "I'm game. What would you like to talk about?" My fingers drummed on the door jamb.

"Everybody we've talked to says you know everyone in town." Frank loomed over me.

A fluttering pink scarf caught the corner of my eye. Alex stepped out onto her front porch. She seemed to stare at the two men for a moment and then disappeared back through the door.

My mouth opened. I snapped it shut.

Bud's head swiveled, and his eyes examined the house next door. "That new dame lives there, doesn't she?" He pulled a piece of paper from his wallet. "Alex Danford. She's someone we'd like to meet."

"Alex is very nice. Why do you want to get to know her?"

Scarface gave me a sinister smile. "We like to cross people off our list."

"I'm pleased you stopped by to chat. I need to be getting back inside now."

"Not so fast. I think we could help each other." Frank leaned on the door.

"Help each other?" I gulped.

"Yeah. The cops think your boyfriend's mother murdered our boss."

"That's true."

"We aren't sure that she did. So it's in our best interest—" he pointed at my chest and then back at himself—"to make sure. Let's pool our resources."

Bud leaned toward me. "Yeah. We don't want to see no travesty of justice done here. You should help us, lady."

I tried to back away, but there was no room, and Frank's hand was on the door. "I'm sure we can work something out. Why don't you come back later when Rob's here, and we can all talk."

"We don't need him. You're the one we want. You're the one with contacts." Bud squeezed onto the top step.

Jay's car pulled up in front of my house. He exited and strolled toward us. "Can I help you, gentlemen?"

"Just talking to the lady, officer. Getting to know the neighborhood." He nodded toward me and whispered, "We're not done here."

Bud started down the stairs. Frank followed until they were on the lawn. He turned to Jay. "Was there anything else you wanted, officer?"

"Nope." Jay stared at them with his arms crossed at the bottom of the stairs. He tossed over his shoulder, "You okay, Merry?"

"Fine."

Frank and Bud got into their car and left.

Jay climbed the stairs to the stoop. "What's going on. What did those two want?"

My knees weakened, and I almost fell. Jay grabbed my arm and steered me into the house, where I collapsed onto one of the chairs. "Thank goodness you showed up when you did."

He crouched next to me. "You look pale. Can I get you some water?"

"In a minute. Let me catch my breath." I rubbed my neck.

"You need to leave investigating to the police. We're trained to handle those kinds of people."

I looked up. "Were you driving by and saw them?"

"Your neighbor called. She thought they might have been threatening you."

"I feel better now." I stood. "Coffee?"

"I wouldn't say no to a cup."

I pressed the button on the coffee machine. "I think I have some cookies here somewhere." I pulled out the jar and set it on the table.

The back door opened, and Rob strode in. "Merry, are you okay? I heard Richard's henchmen were here." He hugged me.

"News travels fast. Have a seat. I was about to tell Jay what happened."

He sat opposite Jay and took a cookie from the jar. I passed around coffee. Then I took a deep breath to calm my nerves. "They're not sure that Rob's mother killed Richard. They want me to work with them to identify the real killer."

Rob put down his mug. "They want to work with you? You told them no, right?"

"I didn't get a chance to." I shrugged. "Jay showed up when Alex called the police."

He handed Jay the cookie jar. "Thanks for the quick response time."

Jay put it down. "No problem. I hate to say this, but we know who killed Richard." He pointed toward Rob. "Your mother."

"Did you get the results from the tests on the champagne yet?" Rob sipped his coffee.

"Not yet. The lab's been backlogged. We should get the results at the beginning of next week. And then we'll be able to prove she killed him."

Rob paled.

I took a cookie from the jar. "Wanda isn't the only suspect."

Jay's eyebrow rose. I told him about the Greens. He said, "Just because you think Richard killed their daughter and son-in-law, doesn't mean they killed him."

"You have to admit; it's a big coincidence. Richard kills them, the Greens move to town, Richard's murdered."

"I'll check into it." Jay stood. "Let me know if those two bother you again." He left.

Rob massaged my back. "You okay?"

"I'm not going to lie. I was scared when I saw them at the door. They wanted to come in; I wouldn't let them, but I think we should talk to them again. They may have information we don't."

"But this time, I'll be there. And we'll talk in a public place of our choosing. I'll stop by the motel on my way home and try to arrange something." He kissed me before he left.

I finished my cookie and eyed the overripe bananas. *Time to make banana bread.* I assembled everything and stuck it in the oven. Then I threw in a load of wash and picked up the dust rag in the living room. I made a quick pass through the dining room with it. The next stop was my office. I straightened my files. The oven timer rang. I took the bread from the oven and set it on a trivet to cool. Ten minutes later, I plopped it on a plate, put a bow on it, and walked out the door. I trotted up the steps to Alex's back door and knocked.

She opened the door. "Hi, Merry. I hope you're okay. I'm not normally so nosey, but those two looked no-good."

I held out the banana bread. "I'm fine. Thank you."

She lifted the plate and sniffed. "Banana bread, my favorite. No nuts, right?"

"I remembered. Don't worry."

"Would you like to come in?"

"I'd like to get a tour of your greenhouse if that's okay."

"I show it off every chance I get. Let me put this inside." She set the bread down on the kitchen table and joined me. "Now, don't get too excited. The greenhouse isn't that large. I used to have huge ones that I would start all sorts of seeds in."

We strolled to the ornate structure. It was perched on a bluestone paver floor. She said, "The door sticks, so let me go first." She lifted it and turned the knob at the same time. "A little trick you need to know."

A wall of humidity hit me as I walked in. "Wow. It's a lot warmer in here."

The inside of the greenhouse was roughly ten feet by fifteen. There was a large metal table in the middle that boasted bigger pots with exotic leaves. The perimeter was lined with a shelf containing dozens of gray cardboard seed holders. Green seedlings reached from the black dirt, and a narrow walkway ran all the way around the table.

Alex extended her hand. "In the middle, I have my tropical plants. I used to put them in the ground by the pond at my last place, but I thought they'd look good in pots running along the alleyway here. These are canna lilies. They grow six to eight feet tall and have the most marvelous looking spires."

One of them had variegated leaves. The light part almost seemed chartreuse. "This is pretty. What color will its fronds be?"

She looked at the one I was pointing to. "That's a Pretoria. Its blooms are a lovely bright orange." She caressed the leaf. "I love loud colors."

"It will certainly add personality." I made my way farther into the greenhouse and pointed to one of the cardboard containers. "What are these seeds?"

She picked up a notebook. "My diagram." She studied it for a moment. "Oh. Those are carrots. I'm going to put a raised bed in and plant them."

"You are industrious."

"Spring and summer are my busy times. I love to garden."

I wandered down the aisle. One corner held taller plants. I caressed the green leaves. The center and veins were burgundy. "This is beautiful. And are those seeds?" I pointed to a cluster of hairy brown pods.

"They are. The seeds were from last year; I need to remember to clip them off." She checked her chart. "Those plants should grow another inch or two this season alone. They have lovely burgundy flowers." She glanced at her watch. "I hate to cut this short, but I have an appointment."

I followed her out of the greenhouse. "I can't wait to see everything in place." I walked back to my house.

She called out, "Thanks again for the banana bread."

I waved to her as I walked in the back door.

My phone buzzed. Patty had texted me: "Busy?"

"No."

"Is four o'clock too early for wine?"

Ten minutes later, the back door opened. "Do you have cheese too?"

"You're so demanding." I pulled cheese from the refrigerator. "Cheddar okay?"

"Yes, and maybe some crackers." She walked past me, opened the pantry, and held up a box. "Are these all you have?"

"The ones you like are in the back."

She rummaged through. "I could have those since they're already open."

"You don't like them. Why would you eat them?"

"I'm a mom. I eat lots of things other people wouldn't." She found the box and held it up. "Luckily I won't have to today."

I cut slices of cheese and put them on a plate, adding grapes and dried apricots. "Anything else?"

She looked up from depositing the crackers in a bowl. "I don't see any wine."

I bent over the wine refrigerator. "Any preference?"

"Let's do a white and sit outside. It's so nice."

The Pinot Grigio in my hand was soon uncorked. Patty grabbed two wine glasses, and we walked out the door.

We sat, and I poured her a glass of wine. "Where is everyone today?"

"The boys are at a birthday party, Cindy is studying with Jenny at the library, and Patrick wanted me out of the house."

My eyes widened. "Did you do something to annoy him?"

"He's calling his long-lost half-brother for the first time and didn't want me to interrupt him." She swirled the wine. "I wouldn't have. Much."

"Yes, you would have. What are they going to talk about?"

"I don't know. They're strangers who share the same deceased father. I wish I were listening on the other phone." She popped a grape in her mouth and then stood. "I need to pace. Distract me."

I recounted my morning adventure with Scarface and his friend.

"Wow. That was some morning. Are you going to work with them?"

"I think we should. Rob's handling the logistics." I ate a piece of cheese. "And then later, I took a tour of Alex's greenhouse. She has spectacular looking plants, and you should see the heirloom veggie varieties she's growing."

Patty put cheese on a cracker and slid back onto the chair. "What kinds of plants?"

"She's big into tropicals. You know, large leaves, fluffy fronds." I gestured toward the alleyway. "She's going to line the alley with them."

"What kind of tropicals does she have?"

"Pretty ones."

"I was looking for something more specific."

"Let me see—" I tilted my head back. "She said one was a Pretoria, you know, like in South Africa, and there was one with pretty green leaves, a burgundy center, and burgundy veining." I took a sip of wine. "It had the oddest seeds. They were hairy brown pods."

Patty sat up straight in her chair and pulled out her phone.

"Is it Patrick?"

She shook her head and put up her index finger. "Did it look like this?"

"Yes. Ooh. Look at the fronds. Those are going to be great. What is it?"

She scrolled up and handed me the phone back.

"Ricinus communis. Interesting."

She pointed at the common name: castor bean plant.

My mouth dropped. "That's what the poison ricin is made from."

* * *

Rob sat next to me. "You've had a busy day."

"Does this make it better, or worse for your mother?"

"What do you mean?"

"We couldn't figure out where she would get ricin. Now we know my neighbor grows it." I shook my head. "Shouldn't that be illegal? Why do they even sell those plants?"

"It's hard to get the seed pod off. And, when you do, you have to grind up the hulls. Don't forget. People grow all kinds of dangerous things just because they look good. Digitalis, Lily of the Valley, even Yews."

"Yews?"

He placed his hand in mine. "Yes. I could brew you a cup of Yew tea, and you wouldn't last very long."

I pulled away from him. "Since when do you know so much about poisonous plants?"

"I started reading up on them after Mother was arrested." He showed me his phone. "Look. There's an entire garden in England devoted to poisons."

"Alnwick Garden. It says the owner got the idea from the Medici's poison garden. Wow. Some of these plants are quite pretty. I'd be worried about them in my backyard. What if the cats ate them?" I shuddered.

"It says here that they encourage visitors to refrain from touching or smelling these plants."

My phone dinged with a text from Patty: "Patrick's mother is still alive."

I texted back: "I know. She lives in St. Louis."

"His birth mother!"

"Oh. Is he going to meet her?"

"Maybe. She lives in Phoenix. She's 85. Talk later. Wigging out."

I put the phone down and updated Rob.

He said, "Patrick shouldn't wait too long if he wants to meet her. She's not getting any younger."

"I'm sure Patrick's emotions are all over the place right now. I hope he makes the right decision."

"He will. Oh, I scheduled time with your two favorite people, Frank and Bud. We're going to meet them at the Golden Skillet at noon tomorrow. I texted Cheryl. She's going to clear your calendar when she gets in."

"It's Sunday. I hate to make people work on their day off."

"She didn't seem to mind."

"But still."

"Okay. I won't do it again. Do you want to hear what they said?"

I settled against his side. "Shoot."

"They were in the bar attached to the motel. I tried calling their room from the lobby, but no one answered. The desk clerk told me that they had gone in the direction of the bar."

My nose wrinkled. "Is it still as bad as I remember?"

"Probably worse. The dark brown indoor-outdoor carpet looks like it's been there since the fifties."

"It used to be tan with dark brown swirls."

"Then they either replaced it, or you can no longer see the tan parts. From the stench, it's probably the latter." He grimaced. "Anyway, Frank and Bud were at the bar. I bought them both a beer and sat down. Their story is consistent. They don't believe my mother did it, so I need to hear what they have to say. They said that since we're cozy with the police, we may be able to help. That, and the fact that there isn't one person in town you don't know."

I elbowed him. "An exaggeration. I'm sure there are dozens of people I haven't met yet."

"Maybe two. Tops." He stood. "I need to get back. I'll meet you at the restaurant at noon." He leaned down for an extended kiss. "Mm. I've missed that." He strolled out the door.

✳ ✳ ✳

Frank picked up his bacon cheeseburger and took a bite. He mumbled, "This is terrific."

"I'm glad you're enjoying it," I said. "Unfortunately, I have only a limited amount of time today, so I suggest we get down to business."

He put the burger down and wiped his hands on a napkin. "All right. We've been checking into people who are new here. We figured they might have known Richard."

"We already know about the Greens." Rob popped a French fry into his mouth.

Bud's mouth dropped. "How'd you find out?"

"A long story. Suffice it to say we know what happened to their daughter and husband." I dabbed my mouth with a napkin. A thought occurred to me, and my hands started shaking. I stuttered, "Y-Y-You didn't have anything to do with that, did you?"

"Before our time." Frank examined his fingernails.

Rob clutched my hand. "What else do you gentlemen have?"

"We're checking into the ex-wives. Two of them are unaccounted for," Frank said.

"What does that mean?" Rob picked up another fry.

"We know people. Our people went to where the ex-wives should have been. They weren't there." Bud turned toward Rob. "That means they might be here. And since she—" he pointed at me, "knows everyone, we figure she might know if they're here.

CHAPTER 12

J enny was peeling potatoes when I got home from work. A lovely scent of garlic, rosemary, and beef permeated the kitchen. I kissed her cheek. "Something smells wonderful. What are you making?"

"A tenderloin of beef."

"On a Monday night?"

"You work hard. I thought you might need a treat. Especially with everything that's been going on."

My right eyebrow rose. "This is a treat. And thank you. But you can't blame me for being suspicious. You don't normally cook."

Her bottom lip jutted out. "I should help around here more. It's not fair that you do everything."

I pulled her close. "You need to worry about school. I'll worry about everything else." I flipped on the oven light. "That looks great. How did you learn to make it?"

She rolled her eyes. "YouTube, Mom."

"Wish I had that when I was growing up. Want me to set the table?"

"Yes, please. And make the salad too."

I retrieved carrots, celery, and peppers from the fridge, a tomato from the dish, and began chopping. "Anything interesting happen at school today?"

"Nope. All the seniors are going crazy. I can't wait until it's my turn."

"How's studying going for finals?"

"Fine, Mom. I'll be happier the end of next week after school's out." She took the beef from the oven, checked her phone, and tented it. "Now, this needs to rest."

My mouth sagged. My little girl was growing up. I looked around her shoulder. "Yum."

She poked the potatoes with a fork. "Almost done."

I set the table and placed the salad bowl in the middle. Jenny sliced the beef. "Does this look right to you?"

It was medium-rare. Perfect. "Better than I could have done myself."

She beamed. "It wasn't that hard."

I put the potatoes in a bowl. We sat.

"Um, Mom." She deposited salad on her plate.

"Yes?" I put a piece of beef in my mouth. "So good."

She shuffled the potatoes around her plate. "You know how I told you I wasn't going to use Jacob to contact Dad anymore?"

My eyes lifted to hers. "Yes—"

"He convinced me it would be okay."

"And?"

"I talked to Dad and Arianna again today."

"Jenny get to the point."

"They want me to meet them. In London."

My stomach clenched.

"It'd be my first time there. Arianna said it's the best place for fashion, and Dad said it would be good for my college resume to have traveled outside the country. He said they'd take me to Parliament and other historic places."

"I wish they talked to me about it first."

"How? You won't talk to them because you're so worried that the Feds will find out."

I pushed my plate away. "You have to look at colleges this summer."

"We're not going until August. Dad said I could come for June and July. He and Arianna plan to rent a house, so we have a place to stay. Dad said he'd pay."

"Jenny, we can't take money from him. You're putting me in a terrible position."

She stood. "It's always all about you. Well, what about me? I miss him." She ran up the stairs.

I surveyed my wreck of a kitchen and the scarcely eaten beef. Both cats sat by the table, eyes following every move, seemingly hopeful that I would take pity on them and drop some. "No such luck." I stood and started cleaning.

Patty stuck her head in the back door. "Can I come in?" Her eyes widened. "Wow. This is a mess."

"Jenny cooked."

"Impressive. I can barely get Cindy to pour her own cereal." Patty took a piece of beef and ate it. "This is good. We'll have to have her cook for us." Her gaze raked the room. "You'll need to come too so that you can clean up."

"Don't just stand there; help me."

Between the two of us, we soon had the kitchen under control. I poured two cups of coffee, retrieved the cookie jar, and we sat at the table. I handed her a mug. "So why are you here?"

"Patrick is driving me nuts. He's vacillating about reaching out to his mother."

"What's the problem?" I pushed the cookie jar toward Patty.

She took one out and laid it on a napkin. "He's worried she won't want to meet him. His adoptive mother has paperwork she received when he was born. He's hopeful that it will mention if she wanted future contact or not."

"Is she going to mail it to him? Or fax it? She has a smartphone; can't she take a picture and text it to him?"

"His mother still relies on us to set the time on the VCR. And yes, she still has a VCR. Patrick's going to drive down this weekend to pick it up."

I pulled the jar toward me and extracted an oatmeal raisin. "Are you going to go with him?"

"Bundling the kids in the car for a six-hour drive does not sound like my idea of fun." She sipped her coffee. "But who knows, maybe he'll take one of the four with him. There is hope in the world."

"Why is he still worried?"

"His half-brother thinks it's a bad idea. Even though she's not his mother, he visits her twice a year. He says she's frail, and he's afraid what the shock might do to her."

"I could see that being a concern. But it's only a problem if she said she didn't want future contact."

Patty dumped her remaining coffee in the sink. "Any wine open?"

"Some of that white we were drinking last night."

Her head disappeared into the refrigerator. She held up the bottle. "You want some?"

I motioned with my hand to bring it on. She poured two glasses and handed me one. "So what's new in your world?"

"Drew and Arianna want Jenny to come to stay with them in London this summer."

Her mouth dropped. "Isn't Drew still on the run? Should she even be talking to him?"

I rubbed my neck, stood, and retrieved two antacids. I chewed them.

"Should you have those with wine?"

I drank water and returned to my seat. "Satisfied?" I sipped the wine. "It really annoys me. He's the one who's wanted by the FBI. I'm not sure why my daughter thinks I'm the bad guy."

"You're closer."

"I'm also the person standing between her and London. He used the 'it will help your college resume' card."

"Jerk." She dipped part of the cookie into the wine and ate it.

My eyebrow rose.

"It's not bad. So what are you going to do?"

I groaned. "I'm not sure. He offered to pay the airfare, but we can't accept what might be stolen funds. So that means if Jenny goes, I'll have to pay. And we still need to tour colleges. That's going to take money. Not to mention actually paying for college." I face-palmed.

She rubbed my arm. "Isn't the business going well?"

I lifted my head. "Business is fine. I want to make sure we're doing the right thing."

She topped off our glasses. "I know you. You'll do the right thing. There's one way we can save money—"

"Lay it on me."

"If Cindy and Jenny end up interested in the same schools, we could alternate who's taking them for visits."

"That's a good idea."

"But it doesn't help you with the Drew issue."

"No. It doesn't."

* * *

I walked into the kitchen on Friday night, and the front doorbell rang.

"I'll get it," Jenny yelled as she tromped down the stairs. The door squeaked open. Jenny said, "Ms. Jenson. What are you doing here?"

I hurried down the hall. Rob's sister, Elizabeth, stood in the entry, a small suitcase by her feet. She hugged me. After a beat, I stepped back. "It's good to see you, but—Rob must have forgotten to tell me you were coming."

"He doesn't know. Mom wanted me to keep it quiet. She has some sort of surprise brewing. She's made reservations for dinner tomorrow for all of us."

Jenny edged away from the door. "All of us?"

Elizabeth touched Jenny's nose with her forefinger. "Yes, everyone. Including you."

Jenny frowned and looked at me. "Do I have to go?"

"Let me find out more about what's going on, and then I'll give you an answer."

Jenny lifted Elizabeth's suitcase. "Are you staying with us, Ms. Jenson?"

"Since Mom's still with Rob, I'd appreciate the hospitality." Elizabeth smiled.

"You're always welcome," I said.

"I'll take your suitcase up to your room." Jenny bounded up the stairs, bag in tow.

"Let's go into the kitchen. Are you hungry?"

"I wouldn't mind a snack."

I took out celery and carrot sticks, along with hummus, and arrayed them on the counter.

She smiled. "Just what I needed."

I uncorked a bottle of wine and handed her a glass. "So what's going on?"

"You know as much as I do. Mom told me there was a plane ticket waiting for me at the airport and that I needed to pack. She told me to bring something dressy for tomorrow night. Apparently, a limo will pick us up at six. So, here I am, as requested."

"I wonder when she's going to tell Rob."

Elizabeth shrugged.

There was a quick rap on the back door, and Rob walked in. His mouth dropped when he saw his sister. They hugged, and he asked, "What are you doing here?"

"You could sound happier."

"I am happy. But I'm worried."

"Mom sent me a ticket. She wanted me to be at some shindig tomorrow."

Rob poured wine and leaned against the counter. He lifted the glass. "What shindig?"

"Something at a veterinarian's house. I had to laugh. You know how Mom feels about animals."

Rob groaned and brought his sister up-to-date. Elizabeth said, "I can't believe she's already on to another man. And she was seeing him before Richard died." She sipped her wine. "What do the police think about all this?"

Rob picked up a carrot stick. "It's made them even more certain they have the right person."

"What do you think is happening tomorrow night?" I dipped celery into the hummus.

Rob rubbed his eyes. "I don't even want to speculate."

* * *

Jenny sat on my bed. She wore a lovely azure empire waist dress that came to mid-thigh. I had opted for a knee-length, sleeveless midnight blue dress with a squared-off neckline. I donned the sapphire necklace Rob surprised me with at Christmas.

Jenny stood and walked to my side. "You look so pretty. What did you decide about me going to London?" She hugged me. "It would be so much fun."

"I'm still thinking about it. I know I have to make a decision soon." I turned her face to mine. "Let's try and enjoy this evening. We have to support Rob."

"Isn't it enough that you'll be there?"

"Who made you blueberry pancakes? Who hasn't missed one basketball game? Who offered to take you car shopping?"

She groaned. "Mr. Jenson."

I picked up my evening bag and gestured for Jenny to precede me out the door. We strolled downstairs. Elizabeth was staring out the window. She wore a form-fitting black sheath dress with a rolled neck and v-back. Small diamond studs graced her earlobes.

I joined her at the window. "I love that dress."

She smiled. "It's my go-to little black dress. You look great. And Jenny, you look amazing too."

Jenny flounced onto the sofa. "Thanks."

Elizabeth pointed out the window. "The limo pulled up. It looks like it could fit ten people."

"I've never been in a stretch limo before." Jenny bounded to the window.

Rob climbed the front steps, and I opened the door. He kissed my cheek and lifted the necklace. "Pretty bauble."

I smiled. "Given to me by a lovely fellow."

He said, "Everyone ready to go?"

Jenny ran out the door. "Can't wait."

I laughed. "It was like pulling teeth to get her to go; throw a stretch limo into the mix and now she's ready."

The driver held the door for Jenny. She disappeared inside. A moment later, her head popped back out. "They have a TV. Can I turn it on?"

I raised my eyebrow. The driver nodded and pointed inside. Jenny disappeared again. Elizabeth joined her. Jenny babbled about the size of the TV, and then music drifted out. I turned to Rob. "Are you okay?"

He pulled me close. "As long as you're with me." He extended his hand to the limo. "After you. We may as well get this over with."

I climbed in. There was a long oblong shaped black leather couch. I sat and slid over so Rob could get in. Next to the TV was what looked like a fully stocked bar. A bottle of champagne cooled in a bucket of ice.

Jenny squealed. "This is the best."

The driver got into the front seat and slid open the partition. "There's champagne if you want it, or other drinks. Please settle in. The ride should only take about twenty-five minutes." The partition closed.

Rob turned to Elizabeth and raised his eyebrow. She said, "May as well. Might make the evening more mellow."

He pulled the champagne out and wiped the bottle. It was Dom Perignon. Rob whistled. "Someone has expensive taste." He popped the cork and poured glasses.

Jenny held out her hand. Rob turned to me. I said, "A taste."

He poured a small amount and handed it to her.

I lifted my glass. "What should we drink to?"

Elizabeth said, "Surviving the evening." We toasted.

I sipped champagne. "This is yummy."

Jenny laughed. "The bubbles tickle!"

The limo exited the highway and passed Mac's veterinary office. I took a sip of champagne. "Shouldn't be long now."

The limo turned off the road onto the long drive. The gate opened automatically. Lilac trees in full bloom lined the drive. I said, "How pretty."

Elizabeth agreed, "They're gorgeous."

Jenny pressed the button for the window. Their sweet scent filled the air. She said, "I love spring."

The limo passed under the portico to the rear of the expansive Tudor house. A large horse stable was on the left, and a massive garage sat on the right. Directly in front of us was an enormous barn. Twinkle lights outlined the roof, and several large pots overflowed with peonies, tulips, and vivid pink creeping phlox. The driver opened the door with a flourish. As we exited the limo, a server extended a tray full of champagne glasses. Rob, Elizabeth, and I took one.

Jenny bounded out last. "Mom, can I go see the horses?"

"Let's see what's going on first."

Her shoulders drooped. I gave her a side hug. "Later. I promise."

The massive barn door had been slid to the side. A crowd of party-goers was inside and on the patio adjacent to the barn. Tables adorned with crisp white linens, plates on golden chargers, and gleaming crystal glasses filled one portion of the room. The other side held white chairs, leading to an elaborate flower-bedecked archway. A raised platform was immediately behind the arch, and next to the platform was a table with three candles.

Elizabeth's hand clutched Rob's. "I have a bad feeling about this."

Rob's face froze. "You don't think—No. She wouldn't."

A man walked onto the platform holding a musical triangle and striker. He gently struck the triangle to get the crowd's attention. Ushers wove through the crowd urging everyone to take a seat on either side of the aisle. One wearing a white dinner jacket approached Elizabeth. "Family of the bride? Come with me, please."

Jenny's mouth formed a perfect circle. "She's getting married again?"

A string quartet played Pachelbel's Canon in D as Mac and Wanda made their way down the aisle. She wore a knee-length rose color dress that highlighted her slender frame, and Mac wore a navy suit. Rob stared straight ahead as Elizabeth, Jenny, and I turned to watch the procession. A justice of the peace performed the short ceremony, and after the "I dos," he requested Elizabeth and Rob to join the newlyweds by the table with the candles. Rob looked like he was about to refuse, but Elizabeth grabbed his hand and gave a quick tug. They joined the couple.

Wanda said, "These are my children. To celebrate our marriage, they will light candles, which we will use to light our unity candle." The soft strains of Beethoven's Ode to Joy started. Rob's hand shook as he lit his candle. Elizabeth wore a smile that looked frozen. Rob handed the candle to Mac; Elizabeth handed hers to Wanda. Mac and Wanda then lit their unity candle and kissed. By the time Rob came back to the pew, his face was beet red. I took his hand, pulled him closer, and whispered, "Try to hold it together."

He squeezed my hand and tried to arrange his face in a smile as Mac and Wanda traveled down the aisle, greeting people as they walked. Rob turned to me. "I have to leave. I'll see you tomorrow." He slid out the nearest exit, avoiding the crowd of well-wishers at the front.

Elizabeth sank into the chair, her color high as well. "I can't believe it."

"Can we leave now?" Jenny shuffled her feet.

"I'm afraid not. I'm sure Rob took our driver, and we're going to have to tough it out until the limo returns. You can see the horses now if you want." She made a quick exit, and I sat next to Elizabeth. "That was a shock."

"It's so stupid. Who gets married after a few months of knowing someone. And just after your other husband died."

"I'm sorry."

"No need for you to apologize. She's my mother." Elizabeth turned. "The crowd looks like it's moving into the dining area. Better put on our happy faces and make our excuses for Rob."

CHAPTER 13

Wanda and her new husband Mac hosted a small wedding brunch the next day in the conservatory attached to Mac's house. Towering topiaries flanked either side of the entrance.

Rob flinched when I touched his arm. "They're starting brunch. We should go in."

"I can't believe she went through with it." He paced the flagstone patio.

"I'm sorry. I know it's disappointing—"

"Disappointing?" His nostrils flared. "Is that what you think this is? She's been arrested for the murder of one husband, and before his body's even cold she's married again!" His hand hit his thigh. "It's stupid, that's what it is."

I rubbed his back. "I know you're mad, but you're going to have to calm down. There are other guests here."

He took a deep breath, and then another. His hands stopped shaking. "I'll be in shortly. I need a moment to get myself under control." He stalked away.

I inspected the ivy trailing from the topiary. It was impressive how they got it to curve into a green ball; it looked so manicured. I glanced at Rob's back. It wasn't as rigid as it had been. Maybe he was getting calmer. I walked into the conservatory.

Mac hurried toward me. He extended his hand, and I shook it. His other hand covered mine. "Isn't Rob with you?" He frowned.

"He's here. He wanted to have a quick look at the horses. He'll be here in a minute."

"Oh, good. His mother would have been so disappointed if he hadn't come." Mac's shoulders relaxed.

Rob entered and strode to meet us. He extended his hand. "Congratulations and welcome to the family. I'm sorry I left in such a rush last night. Stomach trouble."

I put my arm around Rob. All his muscles were tense again. I rubbed his back.

A smile split Mac's face. "That's too bad. Your mother thought that maybe you were upset about the wedding."

Rob grimaced. "Not at all."

Mac extended his arm. "Have a seat. They're about to serve."

Rob and I took our seats between Jenny and Elizabeth. Rob leaned toward Elizabeth and said, "Are we having fun yet?"

She punched his arm. "Not now."

Mac stood and clinked his glass. "If I could have your attention please." He pulled Wanda to her feet and faced her. "I'm so happy to share my life and my happiness with my lovely new wife. To Wanda."

The group murmured, "To Wanda."

I sipped my mimosa. Rob put his down. He whispered. "Not drinking to that."

The servers came out with silver-covered dishes and placed them in front of us. With a flourish, they removed the covers. Jenny smiled. "Eggs Benedict. My favorite."

Rob turned to her. "I thought pancakes were your favorite."

She cut into the egg. "Only when you make them."

A smile lit his face.

I stood and walked to the sideboard. There were several platters, including one that had smoked salmon artfully arranged into roses. I put a bagel onto a plate and two of the salmon slices and rejoined the table.

Elizabeth looked up. "Ooh. Can I have a piece of salmon?"

"Yes. And you can have half of the bagel too."

"When you and Rob get married, you'll be my favorite sister-in-law."

I handed her the plate.

Rob stood. "I don't feel much like eating. I think I'll walk around the conservatory."

"Do you want me to come with you?"

"No. You eat."

He wandered off, inspecting the myriad of plants under the dome. I returned my focus to the plate. A butterfly flew past and landed on Elizabeth's shoulder. I was about to point it out to her when I noticed Rob. He was on the other side of the conservatory standing stock still. His face was ashen. I hurried to his side. "What's wrong?"

With his arm glued to his side, he lifted his finger and pointed. Two rows back was an excellent specimen of Ricinus communis.

My mouth dropped. "Why is everyone growing castor bean plants when they're so poisonous?"

* * *

"I'm so full. I don't think I'll ever eat again." I sank back against my couch cushions.

"Say what you want, that man knows how to feed people." Elizabeth's sock-clad feet were stretched out onto the coffee table.

Rob grunted. "His chef feeds people." He turned to me. "Mind if I make myself a sandwich?"

I swept my arm toward the kitchen. "Be my guest."

Jenny pushed herself off the chair. "I'm stuffed too. I'll be up in my room if anyone needs me." She ran up the stairs.

Elizabeth rubbed her eyes. "I can't believe I have to fly back tonight."

"You're welcome to stay."

"That's sweet of you, but I have patients tomorrow." She rolled her shoulders. "What a mess."

Rob walked back in carrying a sandwich and cola. "Last chance. Anyone want anything?"

Elizabeth and I groaned in unison.

"I'll take that to be a no." He sat. "What are we going to do?"

Elizabeth turned toward him. "Not much we can do. We need to ride it out, like the other ones."

"What if he ends up dead, like the last one?" He took a bite of the sandwich.

Elizabeth sat up. "What on earth do you mean?"

Rob told her about the castor bean plants.

She blanched. "You don't think—"

"I'm not sure what to think. She was the only one in the hotel room with him, and we now know she had access to poison. Maybe she was tired of waiting to inherit."

"She was only married for two years. Kind of a short time to get tired of someone." Elizabeth clutched her stomach. "I may be sick."

"I have peppermint tea. That might help." I started to stand.

She put her hand out to stop me. "That's kind of you, but I don't think it will." She turned to Rob. "What do you think we should do?"

"As much as it pains me to say this, we're going to find out if she did it. And if she did, we're going to turn her in to the police." He rubbed his neck.

Elizabeth fell back against the cushions. "I pray it doesn't come to that."

* * *

Patty and I finished lunch at Delightful Bites. I took a sip of coffee. "So now you're up-to-date. It was a heck of a weekend, and I'm thankful it's over."

129

Patty leaned closer and whispered, "Does Rob think his mother did it?"

"He's afraid she did. Remember the night of that awful storm?"

"How could I forget? We ended up with all four kids in bed with us, and we have a queen size mattress."

"Wanda met me in the basement when I was checking the fuses—"

"And?"

"Her feet were wet. Why would her feet have been wet?"

"No idea." Patty lifted the iced Frappuccino to her lips.

"What if she snuck over to Alex's greenhouse that night? The sound of the storm would have hidden the sound of the back door squeaking."

"How would she have known that Alex had castor bean plants in her greenhouse?"

I drummed my fingers on the table and then lifted my forefinger. "Alex told me she had been giving tours. A lot of people were interested in what she was growing. What if Wanda was one of them?"

"But I remember when Wanda met Alex at Ed and Andy's party. Neither of them mentioned that they'd met before."

"True." I leaned back in my chair. "Back to square one."

Rob and I were clearing up the kitchen after dinner. There was a knock at the back door, and Jay walked in. "Am I interrupting anything?"

"No. Would you like coffee?" I loaded the last dish into the dishwasher.

"Of course." He sat at the table Rob wiped off.

Rob retrieved the cookie jar and handed it to Jay. "What's up?"

"We finally got the toxicology report on the champagne."

My neck grew tight. "And."

"It was clean. There was no ricin in the glasses, the champagne, or anywhere else in the room."

Rob sank onto a chair. "Thank God. So my mother didn't kill him."

Jay held up his finger. "I didn't say that. I said that she didn't kill him with the champagne. The Doc told me that Richard would be having symptoms as early as four hours after being exposed, and as late as twenty-four. "

"When else would she have had a chance to give him the ricin? We went to dinner that night. No one else got sick. And she was staying here. Richard was at Rob's. She couldn't have done it." I smiled and handed Jay a mug.

"That's what we're going to have to work out. I still think she's guilty." He turned to Rob. "You said you didn't know that your mother and Richard had gotten back together the night he died."

Rob gave a slow nod. "That's true."

"So they could have seen each other earlier in the day, and you two would never have known it." Jay pointed with his cookie at me. "You said she borrowed your car that day."

"Yes—"

"So she could have been anywhere with anyone during the day. Even with Richard."

I broke in. "But they didn't act like they'd seen each other."

"Maybe they're good actors."

Rob chewed the cookie slowly and then drank some coffee. He shook his head. "If they had seen each other earlier in the day, I would have known." He touched my hand. "Remember—she wanted to switch seats with Jenny. Why would she have wanted to do that if they had made up earlier in the day?"

Jay stood. "Didn't you think it was odd that they ended up together that night? Maybe they planned it when they met earlier."

"Not the way she was acting that night." I pulled on my ear. "Although they resolved their differences at warp speed." I turned to

Rob. "They only had a few minutes to talk before we got in the car. I guess that is suspicious."

Rob stood. "Not necessarily. We're forgetting that they could have spoken by phone that night after we got home. We went to dinner early that night. They would have had plenty of time to talk." He retrieved the coffee pot, and I put my hand over my mug; Jay beckoned him forward.

I nodded. "I went to bed early that night. I was catching up on my sleep after the awful storm the night before."

Rob sat down, leaned back in his chair, and crossed his arms over his chest. "See. She didn't do it."

Jay rose. "As far as I'm concerned, she killed her husband." On that note, he walked out the door.

"Your mother was a busy woman." I put my cookie back on the napkin.

Rob's eyebrow rose.

"She had Mac on a string and looked like she was reconciling with Richard."

Jenny ran down the stairs and bounced into the kitchen. "Ooh. Cookies. Yum, I need them." She took one from the jar, poured a glass of milk, and plopped down at the table. "What's up? You both look so serious. Did Detective Ziebold have bad news?"

"Not bad news. Actually, it might be good news," I said. "He told us that the poison wasn't in the champagne or the glasses."

"Oh. That's good." She turned to Rob. "I'm glad your mother didn't kill her husband."

"Thanks. We're trying to figure out when she and Richard agreed to meet at the motel."

"That's easy. She was talking to him on the phone that night. You had zonked out already. I came down for an apple, and she was here—" she motioned toward the table. "It was pretty gross. She was cooing into the phone. She glared at me, so I grabbed an apple and high-tailed it back upstairs."

"Why didn't you tell us this before?"

She tucked one foot up under her; the other swung back and forth. "No one asked. I didn't think it was important. Plus I don't know who she was talking with. Could have been husband number six for all I know."

"Jenny!"

"Kidding. She was talking to number five. She said his name."

"This is serious. You shouldn't joke." I pressed my lips together.

Rob's shoulder's slumped. "It's okay. She's right. It is ridiculous."

I turned Rob's face toward me. "It wasn't in the champagne. They made arrangements to see each other that night, not earlier in the day. Your mother didn't kill him. You have to believe that."

"I guess." The clock chimed. "It's getting late. I should go and call Elizabeth. She's going to want an update. Don't forget; I'm going to the town council meeting tomorrow night." He kissed my cheek and left.

I started putting the mugs in the dishwasher. Jenny crumpled her napkin, threw it out, and brought me her milk glass. "What do you think, Mom?"

"About what?"

"Mrs. Jenson. Do you think she killed number five?"

"I don't know. I hope not, but to be on the safe side, I don't want you to be alone with her."

Jenny barked out a laugh. "No problem. I don't even like being in the same room with her." She ran up the stairs.

I trudged after her, and the cats trailed me. They settled on the bed while I washed my face and brushed my teeth. I climbed in, being careful not to make any sudden movements to spark an attack. My phone beckoned, so I texted Patty: "I'll pick you up at seven-thirty tomorrow night. Going sleuthing."

"I'll be waiting with bated breath, Nancy Drew."

I chuckled, put the phone down, and turned out the light.

* * *

Patty slid into the car. "I dressed for the occasion." She wore a black turtleneck paired with black jeans. She appraised me, and her eyebrow rose. "I guess I needn't have bothered."

I wore a teal polo shirt and white jeans. "They know we're coming."

She put her seatbelt on. "Who knows we're coming?"

I pulled away from the curb. "Richard's goons."

"Ah. Scarface and Big Ears."

"Big Ears?"

"You haven't noticed?"

"No. But now I'm sure I'll be staring." We pulled into the motel parking lot. "I told them to meet us in the lobby."

We strolled in. It was brightly lit like there had been a sale on fluorescent lights. The sparse furniture was bathed in their yellow-tinged glow and looked worn. Even worse, the lobby looked like it hadn't been cleaned in the last decade. Scarface and Big Ears waved to us. We joined them.

I tried to avoid looking at Bud's ears, but it was impossible. Patty was right; they were large. I held out my hand. "Thanks for meeting us."

Scarface said, "The pleasure is all ours. Please have a seat."

Patty sat gingerly. "You think they'd clean occasionally."

I gave the chair a futile swipe and said a silent prayer for my white pants as I sat. "I'm trying to figure out what Richard was doing the last day he was alive. I figured since you gentlemen were business associates of his, you might know—he may have checked in with you."

Big Ears leered at Patty. "The rooms are clean. Once we're done here, we could check it out."

Patty leaned as far away from him as her seat would allow. "I don't think so. I'm married and have four children."

He scooted his chair closer. "That's okay."

Scarface put his hand on Big Ears's arm. "Not now." He turned to me. "Why do you want to know where the boss was that day?"

"I spoke with the detective in charge of the case, and he said that the poison wasn't in the champagne."

Scarface slammed his hand down on the table.

Patty and I jumped.

"I knew it." He turned to Big Ears. "I told you the current wife didn't do it."

I leaned toward Scarface. "So where was Richard that day?"

"He had business to attend to that morning, out of town."

My eyebrow rose.

He shook his finger at me. "You don't need to know anything more than that. Bud and I were with him the whole time. The only time he ate or drank was at a McDonalds. And I'm pretty sure they didn't have any reason to poison him."

Patty wiped the part of the table closest to her with a tissue. Then she put her elbows on the table. "What time did you two leave him? Did he say he was coming back to town? Was he going somewhere else?"

Big Ears held up his hands. "You sure are a feisty one. Those are a lot of questions."

"And?"

Scarface answered, "He said he was going back to town. He had a score to settle with someone. I told him we could help, but he laughed. He said that this was one he could handle all on his own." Scarface turned to Big Ears. "I knew we shouldn't have let him go off by himself."

Big Ears shrugged. "He was the boss. How were we supposed to know what was going to happen?"

I drummed my fingers on the table. "So you don't know who Richard was going to meet?"

"The only thing I know is that it was someone he knew." Scarface leaned back on his chair. "And if I had to guess, I'd say it was someone he knew well."

CHAPTER 14

I dropped Patty home, and since it was still early, I went to Rob's. I gave a quick knock and then let myself in with the key. Rob was half-way to the door. He hugged me. "You are a welcome surprise."

I kissed his cheek. "Where's Wanda?"

"Living with Mac now."

"That's got to be a relief. Does Jay know?" I dropped my purse on a chair.

"Her lawyer cleared it with him before she left town. They let her go because she was still in state and only a couple of towns away. He's alerted their law enforcement to keep an eye on her."

"Isn't she running out of clothes by now?" I frowned. "Come to think of it, I've seen a lot of new outfits recently. Is she buying new?"

"She's not allowed to leave the state, and the employees at Richard's house weren't too happy with her after she gave them notice. So she hired someone from the outside to pack up and send her belongings."

"She gave them notice? While she was out of town?" I shook my head. "Doesn't she care about anything in that house?"

He shrugged. "Probably her clothes and jewelry, and that's what the person she hired shipped back."

I walked past him into the kitchen, and he put his hand on my arm. "Do you know you have dirt on the back of your pants?"

I groaned. "It was the wrong outfit to wear to the Shady Inn."

Rob did a double-take.

"That place is filthy."

He stared at me.

"Patty and I met with Scarface and Big Ears. We wanted to find out if they knew Richard's whereabouts the day he died."

"Big Ears?"

"That's what Patty calls Bud."

Rob's head tilted. "I could see that. I would have gone with you."

I kissed him. "You were busy with work. And I didn't want to wait." I chuckled. "Big Ears wanted Patty to go to his room with him."

"That's not funny. Those guys mean business. You and Patty shouldn't be alone with them. Promise me you won't meet them without me again."

"They're not so bad, especially when you're not alone."

He tilted my face to his. "Promise."

"I promise. Do you have any wine open?"

"White." He walked to the fridge, pulled out the bottle, and poured two glasses. He handed me one. "So what did they have to say?"

"Richard went to see someone that afternoon to settle a score."

"Who?"

"They didn't know. If I had to guess, I'd say it was the Greens."

He rubbed his chin. "Wouldn't the Greens have more of a score to settle with him?"

"True. But who else did he know in town?"

"Who else indeed? I think we'd better find out. Otherwise, Jay will shoehorn the facts to fit my mother."

I sat on the kitchen stool and sipped my wine. "Speaking of whom, I think it's time for a serious chat with Wanda."

"Agreed. And I have the excuse. The people at the cemetery called. Richard's gravestone came in. I'll tell her it wouldn't be appropriate for Mac to come when they place it." He ran his finger down my face. "Do you need to go home right away, or can you stay awhile?"

I glanced at the clock. "I need to leave in an hour; ten at the latest."

He grinned. "Plenty of time." He led me into the bedroom.

* * *

The clock struck ten. I bent over and gave Rob a slow kiss. "See you tomorrow?"

"You bet. After viewing the gravestone, I'll take her to dinner. Will you come?"

I scrolled on my phone. "Jenny's with Jacob's parents for dinner tomorrow, so that would be perfect." I touched his lips with my fingers. "Tomorrow." I let myself out the door.

It was a pleasant stroll home, and I basked in the light of the full moon. *I love this town.* I turned into my driveway. Next door, Alex had her easel set up. I turned left and came up behind her. She was painting the moon and the faint clouds that appeared to be drifting in front of it. "That's lovely."

She jumped. "Oh, Merry. You scared me. I was so focused on painting." She completed another brush stroke. "It's such a lovely night that I thought I'd try my hand at the Flower Moon."

"Is that what's it's called?"

"Yes, in most places, because of the abundance of blooms in May. I remember the last time I painted the Flower Moon. It was three years ago. My husband had a lovely large place, with a very lush formal garden. He must have had four full-time gardeners on staff." She chuckled. "Such a large staff. I set up my easel so that the moon peeked through a pergola bursting with Chinese wisteria. I still remember the lilac-colored tendrils dripping from the wood frame. Such a sweet smell. I miss that house."

I sat on the stone bench beside her. "Why did you leave?"

"I wasn't what he wanted any more. He wanted someone with more class, someone with paint on her fingernails, not under them." She held up her well-used hand. It was mottled with different hued paint, and her fingernails were close-clipped. "Not elegant at all."

"Well, I think your painting is as wonderful as you. Do you still have that picture? I'd love to see it."

She frowned. "He kept that and the house. I was lucky to get my clothes. He even kept the jewelry he gave me. He said they were family heirlooms and should go to his daughter." She shook her head. "He was generous when we were married. I couldn't say the same for when we divorced."

"I'm sorry. That sounds like a rough one."

"At least we married when I was older. We didn't have any children, thank God. Not like you."

"Jenny was the best thing to come out of my marriage. I'm so blessed that I had her."

"I heard your husband was kind of a scoundrel."

"He was. And still is. I don't like to talk about it, but this town certainly does." I stood. "I should be getting in. The painting looks lovely, and I can't wait to see the finished product." I stalked back to my house and in the back door. My hands clenched. *Town gossip.*

Jenny sat at the kitchen table, papers spread about her. I plopped my purse down on the stool. "What are you doing up? It's time for you to be in bed."

Her hair draped her face. "It's this paper I'm working on. I'm almost done, and it's due tomorrow."

I pushed back the curtain of hair and kissed her cheek. "Maybe you should have started on it sooner."

She glared at me. "I did. It's hard. It's about philosophy, and I want to make sure my argument is logical."

"Do you want me to look at it?" I sat next to her.

"No time. Give me fifteen more minutes."

"Okay. Fifteen minutes, and I pull the plug."

She crossed her arms and leaned back from her laptop. "Mom, you're not helping. I can't concentrate while you stare at me."

I stood. "Turn out the lights on your way up."

* * *

Rob and his mother huddled under an umbrella by the gravesite. Even though they shared an umbrella, it looked like they were both going out of their way not to touch. I winced. If it had been my mother and me, we would have had our arms around each other, providing moral and physical support. It was sad that they seemed to have lost whatever affection they used to have.

Wanda snapped. "It's about time you got here. It's raining, and we've been waiting."

"We've only been here for a few minutes. Merry had to come from work; we're lucky that she was able to get away."

The stone read: "Richard R. Franco, beloved father and husband," and included his birth and death dates." It had intricate scrollwork around the edges. I said, "That looks nice."

"Great. We've seen it. Can we go?" Wanda huffed.

"Would you like a few minutes with him? Rob and I can wait over there." I pointed to one of the outbuildings, which had an overhang.

Wanda grabbed the umbrella from Rob and stalked off, muttering, "I didn't even want to come; Rob guilted me into it."

Rob's mouth dropped as the rain started pouring in earnest and water ran down his face. I handed him my umbrella and took his arm. He said, "Would it have killed her to remember her ex-husband for a minute or two?"

I put my arm around his waist. "Maybe it was difficult for her."

"You didn't hear her whining in the car."

We strolled. As we rounded the huge oak before the parking area, Wanda came into view. She was by the passenger side door, tapping her foot. I looked up at Rob. "You didn't unlock the car?"

He gave me a slight smile. "Nope."

I elbowed him. "You had a clear sight-line from where we were standing by the grave. That wasn't very nice."

"Yep."

"Beep it open now."

He pressed the button. The car locks rose. She yanked the door open and hurried into the car. I sat behind Rob as he slid into the driver seat.

Wanda glared at Rob. "If I brought Mac, I would have had our car. He would never have left me standing in the rain." She brushed angrily at the water on her shoes.

Rob ran his fingers through his wet hair. "You did have the umbrella." He started the car. "Is everyone ready for an early dinner?"

I said, "Of course."

Wanda muttered, "You would be."

Rob gave her a sharp glance.

I put my hand on his shoulder. "It's okay."

He pulled into a parking spot at Fiorella's. Wanda emerged from the car, still brushing down the sides of her coat. "I can't believe we went on such a wet day. What was the big rush?"

"I wanted to see how the stone came out."

I broke in, "It looked wonderful. They did a great job."

The hostess led us to a booth, and Rob and I slid in on one side, leaving Wanda the other. The waitress appeared. "What can I get you to drink?"

Rob ordered a bottle of wine while we studied the menu. The waitress returned with it, poured three glasses, and took our order.

I lifted my glass. "To Richard."

Rob clinked his glass to mine. Wanda raised her glass an inch and then drank.

"Mother, there another reason why I wanted us to have dinner. There are questions we need to ask you."

Wanda crossed her arms. "Again?"

"This is serious."

She leaned toward her son. "The poison wasn't in the champagne. That means I didn't do it. Case closed."

I placed my napkin in my lap. "Wanda, we spoke with Detective Ziebold yesterday. He said he's not dropping the charges. He thinks you gave Richard the poison earlier in the day."

"That's silly. I didn't see Richard until dinner that night. We didn't even decide to meet until he phoned me after we returned."

Rob clenched his glass of wine. "Mother, you borrowed Merry's car that day. You were gone all day. And the night before, when the power went out, you were wet. Where had you gone? Did anyone see you? Do you have an alibi?"

"I didn't kill him. Why on earth would I need an alibi?"

Rob's voice rose. "Because you're accused of murder!"

People from other tables turned to look at us. I put a hand on Rob's arm. "Maybe you could lower your voice."

He glared at me, and then his gaze softened. He lifted my hand to his lips. "I'm sorry."

"It's okay."

I took a roll and buttered it. "Wanda, you're going to have to tell us what happened. The police will be questioning you soon, and it would be really good to have your ducks in order. We may be able to help."

She sighed. "Very well. What do you want to know?"

"Let's start at the beginning. Why were you outside the night of that horrible storm?" I passed the rolls to Rob.

"I've always loved storms. I guess I didn't realize how strong that one was until the lightning drew close." She smiled at Rob. "Do you remember sitting in our canvas chairs with the garage door up when it stormed?"

He nodded. "You and Dad would dance barefoot in the driveway. You would get drenched. Elizabeth and I would splash in the puddles. It was fun."

"I was about to get into bed that night when the rain started. Thunder roared in the distance. I tiptoed down the stairs, grabbed an umbrella, and ran out the door. I left the light off, so the backyard stayed dark. The thunder grew stronger. I knew I only had a few minutes. I twirled and twirled under the umbrella. I could almost feel your father's arms around me. Then there was a huge clap of thunder, and lightning hit way to close. The light in the kitchen went out. I decided I had better get in. I heard someone moving downstairs, so I took the kitchen flashlight and went to see what was going on."

Rob rubbed his forehead. "I didn't know you ever thought about those times."

"Every day." Wanda touched his hand.

He pulled his hand away. "If you loved Dad so much, why did you marry again? And so often?"

"Because I needed to. We've been through this before. Your father was the only man I ever really loved. I've liked my other husbands, but in my mind, I've still been faithful to him. Money is important to me."

"But you and Dad didn't have money."

She sat straighter. "No, we didn't. But we had each other, and we had you and Elizabeth. Never underestimate the power of trust in a relationship. It made me strong. I wasn't worried about the future. Then in an instant, in an explosion, your father's life ended. And in a way, so did mine." She wiped a tear from her face and then shrugged. "Water under the bridge. It was up to me to figure out what to do, and I did it. One step after another. You may not like it or approve, but it's my life, and I'm living it the only way I know how."

Rob's mouth sagged. The waitress came with our dinners and placed the plates on the table. Wanda had ordered the salmon, broiled dry. She picked up her fork and then hesitated. She looked up at the waitress. "Would you please get me drawn butter to go on this? I feel the need for a treat."

My eyes grew round. I squeaked, "Butter?"

"I give myself latitude on occasion. And this is one of those occasions."

I tried not to smile as I cut into my chicken parmigiana. "Okay, so you've told us about the night of the storm. What happened the day Richard was killed? Where did you go?"

Her cheeks reddened. "You'll think it awful."

Rob looked up from his steak. "Spill, Mother."

"I went clothes shopping. There's absolutely nothing out here in the hinterlands, so I went into the city. While I was at the store, Mac texted me. He wanted me to meet him for lunch at his house. We had a lovely white wine and a gorgeous red snapper." She cleared her throat. "I returned to Merry's at about four and had a bath. You know the rest."

Rob put his face in his hands. "Mother, please tell me that you did not sleep with Mac and then sleep with Richard later that night?"

"I don't think that's any of your business."

I pushed my meal away. "I'm not very hungry."

"Nor me." Rob put his knife and fork on top of the remainder of his steak.

Wanda pursed her lips and then poured the melted butter on her salmon. She lifted a piece to her lips and ate it. "Mm. Delightful."

* * *

I had a presentation to one of my business clients the next afternoon, so I spent the morning preparing. To make sure I'd focus, I had silenced both my work and personal phones. I took a break mid-morning. As I passed Cheryl on my way to the break room, she held up a finger. "You got a call this morning from Richard's daughter. She wants to come to see Richard's gravestone and wanted to know if she could impose and crash at your place Saturday night."

145

I groaned. "I'm getting a little bit tired of houseguests, but I guess it would be churlish of me to say no. Would you return her call, tell her yes, and get all the particulars?"

I continued to the breakroom and poured myself a large coffee. On my way back to my office, I stopped by several desks to catch up on what was going on. We had brought on a few large clients lately, and I wanted to get a feel for the workload. No one complained too much, so I figured we hadn't used up all our capacity yet.

Rob arrived at noon with a bag in his hands. "I know it's a busy day, so I thought you might want lunch brought in."

"And such a handsome delivery man." I hugged him.

I cleared off my desk, and he and I sat on the same side. I unwrapped the sandwich. "Egg salad on wheat. Perfect."

Rob stared at his sandwich. Sighing, he opened it. "I'm still dealing with last night. I'm relieved that Mother didn't kill her husband, but I'm disturbed that she feels she has to marry for security. She could have lived with me, or Elizabeth."

"You were in your last year of school; Elizabeth was finishing med school. How was she going to do that?"

His chin jutted. "I could have dropped out. I'm sure I could have found something."

I rubbed his back. "Your mom wouldn't have wanted that."

"You're right, but I can't believe she wants the life she's living now."

"Mac seems like a nice man. Maybe they'll stay together. Maybe this is the right fit for her."

"Maybe." He bit into his sandwich and mumbled, "I hope so. Jay called her lawyer. He wanted her to come in for another interview."

"Not surprising."

"It isn't." He massaged the back of his neck. "Enough of this depressing stuff. What's new with you?"

"Kathy Franco's coming back to town this weekend."

Rob's eyebrow rose. "What for?"

"She wants to see her father's stone. She's going to stay with me."

"You must be getting tired of having company."

"You have no idea."

CHAPTER 15

Kathy wheeled her overnight bag into the house. "Thank you for letting me stay tonight. I know it's an imposition, but there weren't a lot of choices. You were kind enough to arrange the funeral, and here I am back again."

"It's no problem. You'll be in the guest room—the one Elizabeth was in. Do you need help?"

"No. I'll be back down in a minute."

I pointed to the rear of the house. "It's such a lovely morning. Let's have coffee out back."

She carried her bag up the stairs.

The coffee made; I poured it into a thermos. Then I grabbed two mugs and a plate of scones. Tray prepared, I carried it out and set it down on the table. I sat.

Kathy came out of the back door and joined me. "You have a lovely guest room." She paused. "Not that your daughter's room wasn't nice, mind you."

"The guest room isn't overflowing with her stuff. I understand. Coffee?" I held up a mug.

"Yes, please."

I passed her the scones and napkins.

"These look delicious." She turned the plate. "Are they blueberry?"

"Yes." I handed her the coffee mug.

She sighed. "It's so peaceful here. I love your backyard. So many birds, and your garden's lovely."

"I had to place the feeders and the water fountain strategically. My cats can be killers. This arrangement seems to be working well." I surveyed the yard with satisfaction.

Alex's head appeared over the garden gate. "I thought I heard voices. Am I interrupting?"

I stood. "Not at all. Would you like coffee? I'll grab another chair. Oh, where are my manners? This is Kathy Franco, Richard's daughter."

Alex shook Kathy's hand. "Nice to meet you. I'm so sorry for your loss." She waited for a beat. "No, I can't stay. I wanted to invite you, Jenny, and Rob to dinner tomorrow night." She extended her hand toward the rear of my property. "Andy and Ed will be there." She hesitated. "And Kathy, of course, you're welcome too."

Kathy shook her head. "Unfortunately, I'm leaving tomorrow morning. I just came in to see Dad's headstone."

I said, "Let me check with Rob. I'll get back to you tonight."

Alex waved as she ducked back through the gate. Courvoisier leaped up onto Kathy's armrest.

I said, "Uh-oh. Somebody wants to be petted. Shall I take her inside?"

"No. I like cats."

I sat back down.

Kathy stared at Alex's back. "It sounds weird, but I think I've seen that woman before." She shook her head. "It'll come to me. And now, I should do what I came to do. I'm sorry to move you, Courvoisier." She stood, and the cat jumped off the chair.

"Do you need a ride?"

"I'd rather be alone. If I remember correctly, the cemetery isn't that far from here."

"It's not. Take a right out of the driveway, and you'll see it, about a half a mile down the road."

"I'll see you later." She strolled out the garden gate.

I finished my coffee and decided to dust. Putting on vintage Heart, I rocked it out downstairs, swiping as I went. Satisfied that no mote had been left, I put away the dust rag. The clock chimed one, as I deposited a load of laundry into the washing machine. I wandered to the living room window and peered out. A few people were out walking, but not my guest of the moment. *I wonder where she is.*

Two hours later, there was a rap at the front door. Kathy stood on the stoop, looking exhausted. I opened the door. "Are you okay? It must have been tough seeing your father's grave."

She walked past me and sank onto the sofa. "It wasn't seeing Dad's grave, though that was sad. I stopped by the motel. I wanted to see if Dad's 'associates' had found anything new. I knocked and knocked on the door to their room. Their car was outside. The desk clerk wasn't too happy, but I made him open the door. They were dead."

"Dead? How? They were big guys."

"Shot. They looked like they had been dead for a while. Can I get a small vodka on ice, if you have it?"

"Of course. Just give me a second." I rushed into the kitchen, put ice, vodka, and two olives into a glass. I walked back into the living room. She had her eyes closed, her head resting against the couch. "Here you go."

"Thanks. It was such a shock. This is the first time I've ever seen a dead body that hasn't been in a casket. And hopefully, it will be the last." She sipped her drink. "Thanks for this and the olives."

I sank onto the sofa next to her. "What do the police think happened?"

"They didn't say. I think they were as surprised as I was."

"Frank and Bud had been asking a lot of questions. People in town knew they were investigating what happened to your father. Maybe they asked the wrong question of the wrong person."

She shuddered. "Dad and now them. Maybe it has something to do with his business."

There was a rap at the back door, and Rob called out, "Anyone home?"

"In here."

He rounded the corner. "Did you hear about Frank and Bud?"

"Yes. Kathy was filling me in. She was the one who found them."

He sat on one of the chairs. "Were they poisoned?"

"Nope. Shot." She gulped the vodka, finishing it.

I stood. "Would you like some more?"

She shook her head. "Probably not a good idea." She popped one of the olives into her mouth and rose. "I need to lie down for a bit." She wandered up the stairs.

"I'm going to go to the police station. I want to find out what's going on. Dinner here tonight? I'll bring takeout." Rob opened the door.

"Your mother doesn't have a gun, does she?"

"Not to my knowledge, but I'm finding that doesn't mean a lot." He left.

I ambled around the house aimlessly, until I finally settled on the sofa. I couldn't believe that Rob's mother shot Frank and Bud. It was so pointless. *What a mess.* I picked up my book in the hope it would distract me. After an hour or so, an upstairs door opened. Kathy made her way down the steps and sat next to me. "I feel terrible. I forgot to thank you for arranging for Dad's stone. It was lovely, just like the sketch you sent before it was carved. I sat there for a while on a bench, thinking about my dad. There were fun times mixed in with the bad. I remembered when I was fifteen, and he took me to Aruba. I learned to surf, and he learned to keep his mouth closed when he fell off the board." She laughed, and then her hand flew to her mouth. "That wasn't appropriate."

"It's been a difficult day for you."

"I probably owe Wanda an apology."

"What for?" I closed my book.

"Detective Ziebold said the poison wasn't in the champagne. I guess that means that she didn't do it."

I squirmed. "I know this has been a terrible day for you, but there's something you should know. Especially if you're going to see her again." I coughed. "Um, you see, Wanda remarried."

"What? How is that even possible? We put Dad in the ground a few weeks ago. His stone was just delivered! That woman is a piece of work." Kathy's face reddened.

I mumbled. "You have no idea."

She stood. "Dad wasn't the best man in the world, but you'd think she'd show some respect. The staff at his house told me she'd given them notice. Soon she'll probably sell it, and it will be like he never existed. She got most of my mother's jewelry, you know." Her lips quivered. "Now I'll have two parents who disappeared. I'm going to take a shower. I'll be down for dinner."

Before I could say a word, she shot up the stairs.

✳ ✳ ✳

Kathy came back down at six. "I'm sorry I left in such a snit."

"It was a shock, I'm sure. I'm sorry I had to be the one to tell you." My foot swung back and forth, betraying my nervousness. "Rob's bringing takeout tonight. We thought you probably wouldn't want to go out to dinner. I hope it's okay that he's going to be here."

"Merry, I don't blame Rob. That would be like blaming me for stuff my dad did."

My shoulders relaxed. "Good. So you'll join us?"

"Yes. Although I feel bad crashing your date night."

"We're not seventeen." I opened the fridge. "Wine?"

"Yes, please." Her eyebrows tightened. "Ever since this morning, I've been trying to think of where I know your neighbor from. It's driving me crazy."

"She was a surfer in California if that helps."

Kathy shook her head. "It's the strangest thing. I don't think I've ever actually met her before. It's like I've only seen her from afar—" she paused, "or in a photo."

I poured the wine. As she reached for a glass, she stopped mid-reach and pulled out her phone. "That's it."

"What?"

"It was a photo. Dad sent me a picture of his Las Vegas wedding. I'm ninety-nine percent positive Alex was his fifth wife—the one before Wanda." She scrolled on her phone. "I have all his wife photos in a folder." She stiff-armed the phone to me.

She was a few years younger and wore a tailored white suit, versus her usual bohemian chic. It was Alex.

* * *

Kathy left early the next morning, and Rob and I strolled to the ten-thirty mass. I held his hand. "I can't believe Alex was married to Richard. Why do you think she didn't tell us about it?"

"Maybe it was a coincidence, and she didn't want to get drawn into the middle of everything."

"I can tell you one thing. I'm going to ask her about it tonight if I don't see her sooner. Should we tell Jay?"

Rob held the door to the church open for me. "Yes. It's suspicious, it diverts attention away from my mother, and Alex had access to the poison."

Mass went quickly and Father Tom did his usual good job on the sermon. As we were leaving the pew, I noticed Barbara Ziebold with her brood. "Rob, there's Barbara. Do you see Jay?"

He studied the backs of people exiting and then pointed to the side exit on the left. "He went out that door with their oldest."

I crossed the aisle and headed for the closing door. Rob trailed me. I yanked the door open. They had stopped to the side.

Jay's son was leaning against the building, and Jay shook his finger at him. "Even if your ten-year-old brother pinched your leg, it doesn't give you an excuse to haul off and hit him. Especially not in church. Now you are going to march right back in there and apologize to Father Tom and your brother." He held out his hand. "Your phone."

His son stuttered, "My phone?"

"You'll get it back in a week." He shook his finger again. "That is if you control yourself."

His son handed him the phone. Jay slid it into his pocket. He nodded at us. "Meet you by the front in ten minutes."

We strolled to the front of the church. The doors were still open from the exodus after mass. Jay's son's face was mottled, and he shifted from foot to foot as he spoke with Father Tom. Jay motioned for his son to leave, and he sped past us down the stairs. Jay joined us. "Sorry for the delay. What's up?"

Rob stepped forward, "Do you have any more information on the shootings yesterday?"

"On the record, or off?" Jay crossed his arms.

"On preferably, but off if you'll be more forthcoming."

Jay's eyebrow rose. "Off. The coroner is working to pin down a time of death. Her early read is that they had been dead for several days. Now if that's all you needed, I'll be on my way."

I held out my hand to stop him. "You need to hear this." I filled him in on Alex.

"So she was wife number five?"

"It looks that way."

"Thanks for letting me know. I'll swing by on my way home and ask her some questions." He gestured toward his son. "It'll give him more time to settle down."

I watched Jay retreat. "Do you think Alex will be mad at us for telling him? Maybe I should have asked him not to let on that we know."

"Weren't you planning on asking her about it tonight?"

I gave him a lopsided grin. "You're right. She'd have figured it out at that point. I should make something special for dessert to take with us. Maybe then she won't be too mad."

Rob went into my home office to write an article, and I focused on a strawberry cheesecake. It was unfortunate the party wasn't a few weeks later when the strawberries in my garden would be ripe.

Jenny came through the back door. "Something smells good."

"Cheesecake."

"Yum."

"Don't forget we're heading over to Ms. Danford's tonight. And, Jenny, so you're not surprised, we found out that she was also married to Mr. Franco. She was wife number five, right before Rob's mom."

Her mouth dropped. "How did we not know this before?"

I shrugged.

"Awkward." She disappeared up the stairs.

It sure will be.

At five, we walked out the back door. Rob carried two bottles of wine, and I toted the cheesecake. Alex met us at her back door, and I handed her the dessert.

She lifted it. "This looks wonderful. I'll pop it in the fridge." We followed her into the house.

She pointed toward a makeshift bar she had set up on the counter. "Jenny, soda and ice are over there. And, Rob, you can put the wine down there too. Andy and Ed should be over in a minute—" There was a knock at the door. She opened it. "Speak of the devil."

Andy kissed her cheek and handed her a bottle of wine. "I hope you were saying good things about us."

"Only the best, as always."

Ed squeezed through with what looked like a Caprese salad. My mouth watered.

Alex pointed toward the backyard. "It's getting a bit crowded for my tiny kitchen, so if everyone could grab a drink, and if a few of you would take those plates, we'll go outside."

Andy uncorked the wine, and Rob poured. Jenny took the artfully arrayed cheese and grape plate, I grabbed the carrots and celery sticks, and Ed brought up the rear with the breadsticks. We deposited the goodies on the sheet-draped picnic table. Mason jars bursting with peonies were positioned down the middle, and Alex had strung twinkle lights from the tree limbs above.

I sniffed one of the jars. "I love peonies. These smell like roses."

"They're my favorites too. Such an elegant flower." She sat on one of the folding chairs. "Might be more comfortable to sit in while we enjoy our cocktails. We'll use the benches for dinner."

Rob carried out glasses; Ed followed him with two bottles. Rob put the tray on the table. Ed held up the wine. "Who wants what?"

Andy, Rob, and I said, "Red."

Alex pointed to the white. "I think I'll have that."

Ed said, "I'll join you."

I chose a carrot stick and sat in one of the chairs. "Everything looks great. You must have been working all day."

"I enjoyed it. It's been a while since I've entertained."

I toasted Alex. "To our fabulous hostess." The others chimed in.

Rob said, "It's such a lovely evening to be outside." He put his glass down. "Alex, did anything interesting happen today?"

I turned toward Alex. Jenny stared at her.

Alex started to shake her head. Then she rubbed her face. "I may as well tell you. Detective Ziebold stopped by this afternoon."

Andy and Ed exchanged a look. Ed put his glass down. "Alex, we're all friends here. You tell us what you want to tell us."

Rob frowned.

"It's been stupid to keep this secret. I didn't want to get wrapped up in all the drama."

"What drama?" Andy chewed a celery stick.

Alex shifted in her seat. "I was married to Richard."

Ed's mouth dropped. "Richard, as in Richard who was married to his mother?" He pointed at Rob. "And Richard, as in Richard who died?"

"Yes. That one."

Jenny leaned toward her. "Why didn't you tell us before?"

Alex's eyes narrowed. "Because I didn't think it was any of your business."

Jenny sat back like she had been slapped.

Alex's face relaxed, and she touched Jenny's hand. "Sorry. I shouldn't be so snippy. I was only married to Richard for a few years. It turned out I wasn't what he was looking for. I think he was searching for someone like his first wife." She paused. "Kathy's mother. The one who disappeared."

She tilted her head toward Rob. "I was surprised when your mother came to visit. It was such a coincidence. And then I ran into Richard. I was getting a blueberry muffin and coffee at Delightful Bites. I turned around, and there he was." She sighed. "I know we weren't married for very long, but I couldn't believe he didn't recognize me from the back. I asked him if he wanted to have coffee there and catch up." Her brow furrowed. "He had the nerve to suggest that I had followed him; that I wouldn't give him up. He let me know in no uncertain terms that he was through with me and had no regrets divorcing me."

She seemed to have shrunk in her chair. I moved forward in mine. "That must have been hard to hear."

"It was. But he was wrong. I was over him. I have my art, my place here, and I have new friends." She extended her arm to encompass us. "He threatened me. He didn't like the fact that I had moved in next to

Merry. He told me that if I didn't leave here, I'd be sorry. I was shaking when he walked away." She took a long drink of wine.

Everyone seemed frozen to their chairs. I stood, walked to Alex, and squatted next to her. "He's gone now, so he can't threaten you any longer."

"It's fine. I'm fine." She stood and squared her shoulders. "And now, if someone could help me bring out the food?"

Jenny and Andy jumped from their seats and went with Alex into the kitchen. I turned to Rob. "I'm sorry that happened to her. She seems like such a nice person."

Ed said, "There's something strange about that story."

My head snapped toward him. "Other than the fact that Richard was not a nice guy?"

"That. And, more importantly, if all that happened in line at Delightful Bites, how come this is the first any of us has heard about it?"

CHAPTER 16

I strolled to work the next morning. Alex seemed like such a kind, sweet person. Why would she have lied about running into Richard at Delightful Bites? Maybe it was a slow day when they had their confrontation. I stopped. Who was I kidding? Even on the slowest day, someone would have noticed. This town's gossip mill was more efficient than a Six Sigma assembly line. I pulled out my phone and texted Patty: "Lunch today?"

"Meet you at noon: Delightful Bites."

I tucked the phone back in my purse and opened the door to the office. My day began with a regularly scheduled staff meeting. Everyone gave an update on the progress of our customers' storm claims. I made a note to follow up on the outstanding ones. Next, the party planners told us their ideas for our Customer Appreciation day. They suggested renting a shelter at a local state park and cooking an assortment of hot dogs and hamburgers. "I love it. Full disclosure, I play a mean game of corn hole."

They laughed.

I continued. "Sign-up sheets will be placed on the bulletin board. Please use it so we can get an idea of how many games to bring. Also, I'll be cooking my divine chocolate cupcakes, so don't forget to get back to Cheryl on how many of your family members can make it."

There were a few more reminders on my list. After the meeting was over, there were bookkeeping tasks to accomplish, and then finally, it was time for lunch with Patty. I sauntered down the street; she had already claimed one of the tables outside. I waved as I went in to order lunch. The special was a broccoli and cheddar quiche. I chose that and iced tea. I retrieved the drink and joined Patty. "I'm glad you were able to snag an outside table. It's so nice out."

"It is. I haven't seen you in a while. What's new?"

"Richard wasn't poisoned—"

"With the champagne. Yeah, I know." She sniffed. "Old news."

"Scarface and Big Ears were killed yesterday."

"Heard that."

"You're tough. How about this? Alex, my next-door neighbor, was marriage number five for Richard Franco."

Patty's mouth gaped.

"Not a good look for you." I chuckled.

"How did we not know that?"

"Jenny's exact question. We're usually better than this, which leads me to what I wanted to ask you about."

Patty leaned closer to me. "What?"

"Did you hear anything about an argument between Alex and Richard here at Delightful Bites?"

Patty shook her head. "Nope. And I'm pretty tied in. If a newcomer and a stranger fought here, I would have heard about it. Even you would have heard about it."

"You make it sound like I'm out of the loop."

"If the Cheerio fits..."

Gary Johnson, the owner of Delightful Bites, pushed the door open with his hip. He made his way toward us. "Merry, you had the quiche, and Patty the tuna salad plate?"

"Right," I said.

He put the plates down.

"Do you have a minute?"

"What's up?"

"Do you remember Alex Danford and Richard Franco having words here a few weeks ago?"

He frowned. "A few weeks ago? Alex was in the other day—" He looked up at the sky for a moment and then shook his head. "Nope. Don't recall. We've been pretty busy though, so as long as they weren't swinging at one another, I might not have noticed." He glanced through the window. "Line's starting up again. Got to go."

I cut into the quiche. "It's weird. Alex told a very detailed story. I can't believe she made it up."

Patty put dressing on her salad and mixed it. "People make up stories all the time. You should know that."

"I do. I'm not Pollyanna."

"I didn't say you were. Want to hear the latest on Patrick's saga?"

I put my fork down. "Of course."

"He went to see his adoptive mother this past weekend."

"And? What did the letter say?"

"Patrick didn't want to open it there. He wanted to have all of us around him. So he drove back, and we opened the letter on Sunday afternoon. It was a lovely letter. His mother talked about how difficult the decision was to put him up for adoption. She also said that if he ever wanted to find her, seeing him again would be the greatest joy." Patty dug into her salad.

I sat back in my chair. "All these years. His mother will be so happy when she finds out how successful his life has been. What's the plan?"

She sipped her tea. "Patrick's going to fly to Phoenix next month. I told him that I'd be happy to go, but he wants the first visit to be solo. He figures it will be enough of a shock to see him, let alone me and the rest of the brood."

"Will his brother be there?"

"No. Even though it might be simpler to have him do the introductions, Patrick says he's been giving strange vibes." She gripped her fork. "I'm praying that his mother doesn't die before he gets there. He's so close to seeing her again. It would be such a letdown if it didn't happen."

I ripped open a sweetener packet and stirred it into the tea. "If you want to go, I'd be happy to stay with the kids."

She sighed. "I want to go. What if it doesn't work out? Then he's there with no one."

I touched her arm. "It will be fine. She'll hold on until he gets there, and they'll hit it off."

"I hope that's true."

* * *

When I walked down my driveway that evening, Alex was in her backyard, pulling weeds. With a groan, she got to her feet and then waved. "Good day at work?"

"Busy. Your yard looks so much better. When my ex and his girlfriend rented here, they weren't focused on outdoor activities." I climbed the three steps to her backyard.

"They sound like interesting people. But I'm glad they left so I could buy this house."

"Do you have time for a break? How about a glass of wine?"

She took her garden gloves off. "You talked me into it. I have brie I bought today."

"Love brie. Let me drop my things inside and grab the wine. I'll meet you by the chairs." I hurried up the steps and put my purse and briefcase on the chair. I retrieved a bottle of white and two glasses.

I was almost out the door when Jenny walked into the kitchen. "Where are you going? Is Mr. Jenson here?"

"No. I invited Alex over for a glass of wine. She's bringing cheese. You're welcome to join us if you'd like."

"What are we having for dinner?"

"I'll call for a pizza in about a half-hour."

"Sounds good." She bounded back upstairs.

Alex was already seated in one of the chairs when I navigated my way through the door. She made as if to stand, and I said. "I've got it. Don't worry."

She settled back in the chair. "Another lovely night."

I uncorked the wine. "It is. Warm enough to be able to sit outside in comfort, but not too hot so that we're surrounded by bugs." I placed Alex's wine on the table, set mine down, and sat. "This cheese looks scrumptious." I cut a piece, put it on a cracker, and ate it. "Mm. So buttery."

Alex helped herself. "You're right. I'll need to get more."

Loud, continuous beeping ripped through the air. A FedEx truck backed down my driveway. The driver hopped out and knocked at the gate. I said, "Come in," and walked over to greet him.

Jenny ran out the back door and almost collided with me by the gate. The driver flinched. He held an envelope up as if it were a jump ball. "Jennifer March?"

"That's me," Jenny said.

"Sign here." He handed her the envelope and pointed to a place on the tablet. She signed, and he left.

Jenny turned to go back into the house. I put my hand on her arm. "Who's sending you something by FedEx?"

"It's nothing, Mom. Just college-related stuff." She waved to Alex and dashed into the house.

I frowned and sat. "Surely colleges do everything electronically now?"

"One would think." Alex put her wine down. "Do you want to go talk to her? We could do this another evening."

"No. I'm sure everything is fine." I sipped my wine.

"I had to go down to the police station again today."

"Oh?"

"Detective Ziebold wanted to ask me about Richard's employees, the ones who were staying at that motel in town. The Shady Inn?" She spread the brie on a cracker.

"That's right."

"I assured the detective that I didn't even know the gentlemen. Other than that time they bothered you."

"I'm sure they're questioning quite a few people."

"Now it seems like this might have been something related to Richard's business. I always had the feeling it wasn't on the up and up."

"It was such a surprise yesterday when you told us you'd been married to Richard. Was he the husband you told me about? The one who was looking to trade up?"

"Wanda was the new and improved version." She took a sip of her wine. "At least she and I are the same age. I guess it would have been worse if he had thrown me over for a thirty-year-old. It does stick in my craw that she gets everything. My standard of living definitely changed for the worse when he divorced me."

I put more brie on a cracker. "How long were you separated before he married Wanda?"

She gave me a lopsided grin. "I think the door had just hit my butt when she waltzed in. I'd be surprised if Richard's staff even had a chance to change the sheets."

"He seemed to attract high-quality women. What was his secret?"

She stared at the sky, and her voice grew soft. "When times were good, he could make you feel like you were the only person on earth. He showered me with gifts. And you know how you can tell when someone really listens to you?"

I nodded.

"He focused on me. He asked great questions about whatever story I told. I felt cherished."

"That must have been nice."

"It was. But then I experienced his other side. People warned me—past associates and girlfriends of his—but I didn't listen. And then boom. No more sweet Richard. Pain in the neck Richard, take everything from you Richard." She stood. "I'm sorry, all this talk of Richard has put me in a lousy mood. I'll see you again soon." She turned and walked through the gate.

I sipped my wine. Rob strolled into the backyard. "Oh, good. You've already uncorked a bottle."

I pointed toward the kitchen. "You'll have to get yourself a glass. And while you're at it, you may as well bring Alex's in."

"Alex was here?"

"Yes. She told me all about the two sides of Richard."

"Did you ask her why she lied about running into him at Delightful Bites?"

I shook my head. "Didn't get a chance."

He retrieved a glass and poured the wine. I held up mine, and he topped it off. He sat.

Jenny opened the bathroom window. "I'm hungry. Do you mind if I call for the pizza?"

"Go ahead." I turned toward Rob. "Jenny got a FedEx package this afternoon. Who would be sending her something overnight? She had to sign for it too."

"Who sent it?"

"She said it was from a college, but almost everything she's done so far with them has been electronic."

"Sounds like a conversation for dinner."

The pizza arrived about twenty minutes later; Rob paid and brought it into the kitchen. Jenny had already set the table, so I retrieved the salad bowl, and we all sat.

Jenny opened the box. "I'm so hungry. I hope no one minds, but I ordered pepperoni and sausage." She lifted out a hefty slice and deposited it onto her plate. I handed her the salad bowl, and she added that to the side.

Rob took a slice and bit into it. "This hits the spot." He turned to Jenny. "Thanks for putting in the order."

She gave him a thumbs-up, still chewing.

I took a few of the abundant pepperoni pieces off my slice and placed them on Rob's.

His left eyebrow rose.

"Are you objecting to me giving you my excess?"

"No. Not at all. I was surprised you weren't going to eat it."

"It's heavy with all that meat."

Jenny sighed. "Tastes perfect to me."

"Jenny, about that FedEx truck."

She put the slice down. "Does anyone need anything more to drink?" She stood.

"Sit down."

She slid back into her seat and crossed her arms. "What about it?"

"What was in the envelope?"

"I told you. It was college-related."

"Go get it."

She squirmed in her seat. "The pizza will get cold."

"Finish that slice, and I'll put it in the oven to keep warm." I stood, turned the oven on, and slid in the rest of the pie.

Jenny threw the crust on her plate and ran upstairs.

Rob caressed my hand. "Want me to leave?"

"Stay. You only had one slice of pizza. You must still be hungry."

"A little, but this seems like it's important."

Jenny pounded down the stairs and threw the envelope onto the table.

I opened the envelope. Inside was an old fashioned first-class ticket to London, leaving at the end of the following week and returning at the end of July. My mouth dropped. "You said it was from a college. And who even prints airline tickets anymore?"

Her chin jutted. "I said it was college-related. Going to London will make me more well-traveled. Dad said he'd feel better if I had a paper ticket, and he has a travel agent in Brunei who printed it for him."

"We've had this conversation. Your dad's legal situation is precarious at best, and I don't want you getting involved in it. I especially don't want you to accept any money or a ticket from him." My voice rose.

She drew herself up to her full height. "I told you I wanted to see Dad. And I want to see Arianna again. They've rented a place in London. It's all decided."

Heat rushed to my face, and I counted to ten.

Jenny sat down next to me and stroked my arm. "It'll be okay. You'll see. And I'll be back before you even know I'm gone."

She stood and ran back upstairs. I yelled after her, "This is not the end of this discussion!"

I sank back on the chair. "I can't believe this. My daughter wants to visit a man wanted by the Feds."

Rob put his arm around me. "Not just any man. Her father."

I jerked back. "You're on her side?"

He pulled me close. "No. Of course not. But I know that she and Drew grew close when he moved in next door. She got used to having him be part of her life again after the four years he spent in prison."

I groaned and put my head in my hands. "What am I going to do? I can't let her do something that could mar her life forever. She's seventeen, for goodness sakes."

"We'll figure something out. Do you want me to stay?"

"At least take some of the pizza with you." I stood and put two pieces on paper plates that I then wrapped in aluminum foil.

He kissed me and held my face between his hands. "These things have a way of working themselves out."

"One can only hope."

He left, and I put another slice on a plate and brought it up to Jenny. I knocked on her door.

"Come in."

I pushed the door open. She sat at her desk. I handed her the plate and sat on the bed. She bit into the pizza and her eyes closed.

"I know how much you want your relationship with your father to continue. And I don't want to stand in your way. But he's still a wanted man. I can't let you get tangled up into his schemes." I rubbed my forehead. "You have your whole life ahead of you."

"You can't keep me from going."

"We'll talk about it more tomorrow. I've got a massive headache."

I walked out and shut the door. *What am I going to do?*

CHAPTER 17

I shuffled through the door to Delightful Bites the next morning looking for a truly tall cup of java. After tossing and turning the whole night, I hadn't gotten more than an hour or so of sleep.

It was my turn at the counter. I ordered a jumbo coffee and an apple fritter. *Medicinal sugar doesn't count.* The clerk handed me a cup and bag.

I slumped at the coffee station, filling my cup, and stirring in sweetener. Clutching my treat, I nearly plowed into Diedra Green. "I'm so sorry. I should be looking where I'm going."

She held up her hand. "No harm done. Do you have a few minutes? I hate to drink my morning coffee alone, and Kevin had an early appointment."

I checked my watch. "I have twenty minutes, but then I need to leave for a meeting."

She moved to the line. "I'll be back in a few minutes."

I sank onto the chair, opened the bag, and ripped off a piece of the fritter. It was delicious. I tore off another small bite and popped it in my mouth.

Diedra sat opposite me. "Thanks again for waiting. What's new with you?"

My mouth gaped. I had no idea where to start.

She patted my hand. "Are you all right?"

"Teenager problems." I rubbed the back of my neck. *Understatement of the year.*

"I remember those days. Hang in there, they soon pass." She shifted in her seat. "I've meant to call you. Kevin and I want to invite you to our house for dinner. We've finally gotten moved in, and it's starting to look like home. Are you free on Saturday?"

I checked my phone. "I am. I'll need to check with Rob." I texted him. My phone dinged. "He's free too. What time?"

"Sixish?"

I made an entry on my calendar. "It's a date. We look forward to it."

"I can't wait for you to see the garden. We've done a lot."

I glanced at my phone. "Thanks for the chat and the invitation, but I need to get moving."

My shoulders slumped as I walked to the office. If I let Jenny go to London, she'd be leaving the end of next week. For a whole two months.

I walked into my office and shut the door. Then I checked the time difference to Brunei. Pretty late, but not too late. I picked up the phone and scrolled for Drew's number.

He answered on the second ring. "I was wondering how long it was going to take you to call. Did Jenny get the ticket?"

Heat filled my face. "You could have called to warn me."

"I knew you didn't want any contact with us."

I gripped the pencil tightly and doodled a skull and crossbones. The pencil broke, and I threw it across the desk. "I don't even want to be talking to you now. You need to cancel that ticket and call Jenny. I want you to tell her it's not in her best interest to come."

"I'm not going to do that. Arianna's rented a place in her company's name in London and Jenny is going to stay with us. Didn't you see that I'm getting her back in time for your college trips?"

My voice dripped sarcasm. "Thank you for that. What's going to happen if the Feds discover where you are? I thought the whole point of going to Brunei was that they didn't have an extradition treaty."

"That's why everything is in Arianna's company's name. They won't be able to trace anything back to me. I didn't want Jenny to have to come all this way by herself. London's a shorter hop. Maybe she can come to Brunei next year."

I ground my teeth. "What if something goes wrong? Do you want Jenny to get into trouble? She's only seventeen!"

"No need to screech. We're going to have a terrific time, and I promise I'll send her back to you safe and sound."

I slammed the phone down and kicked my desk door shut.

Cheryl knocked and then opened the door. "Everything okay, boss?"

I popped two antacids. "I'm okay."

She came closer. "You're awfully red. Would you like ice water?"

"Yes. That'd be great."

When the door shut behind her, I picked up the phone again and dialed Father Tom. Belinda answered the phone. "Rectory."

"Belinda, it's Merry March. I need to see Father Tom. It's urgent."

Pages ruffled. "I could shift things around. Can you be here at three?"

"Yes. Thank you. I can't tell you what this means to me."

Cheryl walked in with ice water. "You're still awfully red. Would you like me to call the doctor?"

"No. I'll be okay. I need to leave today at two-thirty. Please clear my calendar."

"You got it." She bit her lip. "Are you sure there's nothing—"

"There isn't. Thanks." I studied the papers on my desk, and the door closed. I held the ice water against my cheek and tried to breathe more deeply. Somehow I got work done during the next few hours. At two-thirty, I pulled my purse from the drawer and strode to the church rectory.

Belinda looked up when I walked in. "You're a little early. He's with someone else but should be done soon. Would you like water or tea?"

"Tea would be lovely." I sank onto the damask covered bench. It was usually such a comfortable spot. The afternoon sun shone in the bay window, and the tiger-striped rectory cat snoozed in the alcove. My hands were tightly clasped together. Belinda placed a teacup next to my elbow, and I jumped. "Sorry. I'm not myself today."

"Hopefully, Father Tom can help."

"Thanks for the tea." I lifted the cup to my lips.

Father Tom's door opened, and a parishioner came out. He gave me a small nod as he passed. Belinda said, "You can go in now."

I walked into Father Tom's office and collapsed onto the chair by his desk. I wrung my hands. "Father, I'm not sure what to do."

He walked around his desk and sat in the chair next to me. "Merry, that's not like you. Why don't you start from the beginning?"

"It's Drew."

He sighed. "I had a feeling it might be."

"You know that he left here with the Feds on his heels."

"I heard that."

"Well, he moved to a country where the United States has no extradition treaty."

"Uh-huh."

"Now his girlfriend has rented a place in England, and they want Jenny to come for two months. She got the ticket yesterday."

His kind brown eyes studied me. "That could be problematic."

"I know. What should I do?"

"What are your choices?"

I crossed my legs. The one on top was moving faster than a sped-up pendulum. "I could let her go and pray that nothing happens. I could forbid her to go and have her hate me forever. Or, I could let her go and alert the Feds that Drew is going to be in London. But then she'll see him arrested again. And she'll hate me." I shook my head. "This is awful."

"Let's take them one at a time. What if you let her go?"

"She'll be happy. But what if the Feds find out? Will she be in trouble? If I let her go, I'll feel like a horrible mother. I'll also feel like I'm doing something wrong. That man's a criminal. What about all the new people he swindled?" I rubbed my neck.

He sat back in his chair. "I see. What about the next one?"

"She loves her father. If I don't let her go, she'll see me as the villain."

"And the third?"

"How is my daughter going to feel if I turn in her father? It's probably the right thing to do, but I don't know if I can. I can't believe I'm faced with these miserable choices. That man is truly despicable." I sipped the tea. My hand shook. "What am I going to do?"

"With prayer, you'll arrive at the right decision."

"What do you think I should do Father?"

"As much as I'd like to, I can't decide for you. All I can do is pray with you and hopefully guide you to the right place."

I held up my hands. "What's the right place?"

"I have faith in you, Merry. Your mind is swirling now. You need to find a quiet place to think. No one will be in the church until choir practice at five. I suggest you go there and pray. I think your path will become clearer." He stood. "I have another parishioner waiting. I'll come to the church when I'm done, and if you're still there, we'll talk again. Bless you."

"Thank you for seeing me on such short notice." I stumbled out the door, handing my teacup to Belinda. "Thanks."

I walked the short distance to the church and sat in a pew mid-way up the aisle. I knelt and began to pray. The ritual calmed me, and my breathing slowed. I was able to focus. There was only one real choice. I couldn't let Jenny get on that plane.

I crossed myself and hurried home.

Jenny was studying for her last final at the kitchen table. I sank onto the seat next to her.

She put her pen down. "You look beet red, Mom. Were you out in the sun?"

"No. I've been thinking about this whole trip to London."

Her eyes sparkled. "And you're going to let me go?"

"No, Jenny. It wouldn't be the right thing to do." I put my hand on hers.

She snatched her hand away. "I can't believe you're not going to let me go. He's my dad. And I want to see London. I've been watching videos. It looks amazing."

"I'll take you to London when the time is right. But that time isn't now. I wouldn't be doing my duty as your mother if I let you go."

"You're worried about the Feds finding out."

"I am. I'm also worried about you consorting with someone who is wanted for defrauding innocent people. I tried to shield you, but you remember how bad it was when he was arrested the first time. All of those people who thought he was going to make them rich."

"It was sad he disappointed so many people here in town. And I can't believe he did it again." She grabbed my arm. "Maybe he didn't. Remember innocent until proven guilty."

I held her face in my hands. "Sweetie, he and Arianna fled the country to a place where there is no extradition treaty. He looks guilty."

"Yes, but maybe he isn't. Maybe he knew that they were coming for him and didn't want to go through another trial. He was suspected of murdering two people last year, and he didn't do it. You found out who did. Mistakes happen."

"Honey, if he didn't do it, let him come back here and straighten this mess out. And until he does, you are going nowhere near him."

"You're ruining my life!" She stood, slapped her study material into a stack, and ran up the stairs. A door slammed.

In a weird way, I felt better. The decision had been made, and the initial conversation was past. Now I needed to keep up my strength for the aftermath.

Dinner was a strained affair, and I was only too happy to see my teenager leave the table. The door slammed again. I retrieved a large glass of wine and retreated to my bedroom. Ensconced amid my pillows, I opened the book I had been reading. My phone buzzed from the end table. Rob texted: "You okay? Sorry I couldn't make it tonight."

"Told Jenny she couldn't go to London."

"How did that go?"

"Swimmingly. Talk tomorrow." I signed off with a heart emoji.

He sent me a hug.

Before long, my eyes drooped.

Something was kneading my shoulder. I kept my eyes shut, hoping it would go away. It didn't. I opened them, and Courvoisier's face hovered inches from mine. It was still dark out. "What?" Then I remembered; I hadn't fed the cats before I came upstairs. "I get it. Hold on a minute."

I put on my flip flops and made my way downstairs. Drambuie was dancing around the empty bowl, and Courvoisier joined her. I filled the dishes and gave them fresh water. "Sorry."

I made my way back up the stairs. There was a light on in Jenny's room. I knocked and opened the door. She had a headphone on and looked fascinated by something on her tablet. I pulled one of the earpieces away. "Jenny."

She jumped. "What?"

"It's late. What are you looking at?"

She held the tablet out. She had been facetiming Drew. He waved. I jumped back. "I was telling Dad that you won't let me come. He wants to talk to you."

"It's late, and you have a test tomorrow. Tell him, goodnight."

She sighed. "Attila says I have to go to bed. I'll talk to you soon."

She took the headphones off and put down the tablet. "Happy now?"

"Yes." I stalked out the door, shutting it after me. *This is going to be a mess.*

✳ ✳ ✳

I had several early meetings the next day. Once they were finished, I closed the door to my office and picked up the phone. I set my shoulders and dialed Drew's number.

He answered on the second ring. "Why are you calling so late? And why did you tell Jenny she can't come to London? She wants to see us, and we want to see her. I miss her."

"If you want to see her, come back here."

There was a pause. "That's a problem for me; you know that."

"You have two choices. You can come back here and face the music, or you can stay there and not see your daughter. That's it. It's simple, really."

"You're awfully hard."

"Don't put this on me. You're the one causing this whole mess. She's not coming. End of story. I'll have her mail back the ticket." I hung up. A small smile creased my face. At least that part was done. Now all I had to deal with was Jenny. The smile disappeared.

I texted Patty: "Need pick me up."

"A little early to be drinking."

"Drinking won't help."

"That bad?"

176

"Yes."

"Shopping! You need something new. April and Sandy's store is doing a soft opening this week. The grand opening is next Saturday. Meet you there at four."

"Okay."

Somehow I muddled through the rest of the day. Around four, I left the office and wandered up the street. A new sign hung outside the store. It used to be Shades of Grey. The crisp new sign sported an Eiffel Tower and read: "C'est Magnifique." Patty stood outside near the door. "What happened?"

"Let's talk later. For now, let's shop." We walked into the store. A bell rang as we entered.

April greeted us. "Welcome."

Patty had done a terrific job designing the place. Washed-out black and white wallpaper lined the walls with small Eiffel Towers interspersed with Toulouse-Lautrec images. Clothes were arranged by color and looked vibrant against the walls. I turned slowly, taking it all in. "It's beautiful."

Sandy joined us. "Was there something, in particular, you were looking for?"

I shook my head. "I wanted to see the new store. I do have a dinner I'm going to this Saturday, but it'll be a relaxed affair."

She led me to one of the racks. "This is where we have our more casual wear."

I held up a black and white shirt embossed with cats. "This is nice."

Patty shook her head.

I put it back. She dangled a turquoise blouse, enhanced by small gold flecks, in front of me. "This does great things for your eyes."

I took it from her and stood in front of the mirror. "I do like this. Let me try it on." I ducked into one of the changing rooms.

The bell rang. April said, "Welcome to our store. The grand opening's not until next week, but please have a look around."

Wanda said, "I have an event coming up, and I need something dressy. I would have gone into the city, but I was on my way to my son's and saw your store. Silly really. I'm sure you don't have anything I'll like."

I groaned and leaned against the changing room door. I put on the blouse and walked out. "Hello, Wanda."

She looked me up and down. "Finally you're wearing something that actually looks good on you."

April's mouth gaped. I shrugged. "April meet Wanda Jenson. Wanda is Rob's mother."

Wanda pointed to April. "Merry will take that blouse. Put it on my bill. Now, where do you have your more formal things?"

Sandy took Wanda to the other side of the store. Patty sidled up to me and whispered, "Well at least she's paying for it. That shirt was expensive."

"I noticed." I went into the changing room and put my shirt back on. I came out and handed the new one to April. "I guess I'll take it."

She lined a box with tissue paper and then carefully folded the shirt. She wrapped the box and decorated it with a bow. I picked up the package. "You didn't have to go to all that trouble; you could have just put it in a bag."

"It's more fun this way. When you get home, you'll feel like you received a gift. We do this for everything sold in our store. It makes the shopping experience more special."

I smiled. "I can't wait to wear it."

Wanda walked by on the way to the changing rooms. I touched her arm. "Thanks for the shirt."

"You're welcome." She turned on her heel and shut the changing room door after her.

Patty and I walked out the door. She laughed. "That woman isn't the most pleasant person in the world by a long shot."

I giggled and held up the box. "She is not. But at least I got the shirt as payment for putting up with her. Do you have to get home?"

"No, I still have time."

"Let's get a drink at the Pickled Herring."

We walked in and sat at the bar. Ann came over. "Your usual?"

Patty and I nodded. Then I blurted, "And mozzarella sticks."

"You got it."

Patty set her purse on the bar top. "Spill, what's going on?"

I held up my finger. Ann put two glasses of wine on the counter. I put twenty-five dollars on the bar. "I'm paying tonight." I sipped my wine. "It's Drew," I told her everything that had been going on.

"Wow. I'm sure Jenny's not a happy camper."

"Understatement. Am I doing the wrong thing? Do you think I should let her go?"

She gripped my elbow. "Someone has to be the adult, but it'll be difficult until she gets over it."

My head drooped. "If she ever does."

"She will. She loves you. Though I don't know if I'd forgive you for keeping me from London."

I punched her arm.

"Ow. Kidding."

CHAPTER 18

I knocked on Jenny's door the next morning. Nothing. I knocked again. "I need to speak with you." The door swung open.

"What?"

"Here's a shipping envelope. You need to take the ticket to the Post Office today and send it back. Make sure you get it insured. If your father had purchased an electronic ticket, we wouldn't have to go through all this extra work."

She grabbed the envelope from my hand. "Fine." The door slammed.

"Jenny, it's the right decision."

Silence.

I retreated down the stairs. A cup of coffee later, I felt more at peace with the world. Scrolling through my calendar for the day, I noted that Cheryl had added lunch with Rob. It would be good to see him; I'd been busy the past few days. I gathered my things and headed out the door.

Alex's easel faced the alley. I walked up the slight hill and looked over her shoulder. "Pretty. Your flowers are doing so well."

"Manure. It helps." Her paintbrush never paused.

"I have a question for you."

She dabbed a little more red onto the canvas. "Yes?"

"You said that you argued with Richard at Delightful Bites."

"I don't know that I argued. It was more like Richard telling me off."

I waved my hand. "Whichever. The thing is this town is porous when it comes to secrets. It's surprising that no one seemed to have seen you two there."

"You asked people about me?" She put her paintbrush down.

I put my hand to my chest. "Rob, Ed, and I talked about it the night of your dinner party. We thought it was odd we hadn't heard about it before then." I left out the part where I asked Patty and Gary about the incident.

"I'm disappointed in you, Merry. I thought you were a friend. Richard and I were the first ones there, around six. People in this town aren't up and about by then." She picked up the painting and easel.

"But Gary—"

"Gary wasn't there that morning. His wife wasn't feeling well. That new clerk was there." She snapped her fingers. "Kelly. She didn't last long."

"Oh."

She brushed past on her way into her house.

I stood there for a moment. It could have happened. Either way, she hadn't been upfront about her marriage. My phone buzzed. I jumped. *Time to move.*

The morning seemed sped up. At noon, Cheryl knocked at my door. "You're going to be late for lunch with Rob."

I hurried to the Golden Skillet. Rob waited for me outside. He hugged me. "I've missed you." I relished his embrace for a few beats too long. His green eyes examined me. "Are you all right?"

I let go. "I'm fine. And hungry."

The host showed us to a table. I sat and opened the menu. "I always order the same thing. Today I'm going to get something different." I placed the menu to the side.

He put his down on top of mine. "I saw Jenny going into the post office."

"Good. She must have mailed Drew's ticket back. I thought she'd hold off longer. Hopefully, she'll be more pleasant to be around now that everything's been decided."

"Has it been bad?"

The waitress walked up. My eyes widened. "Kelly, right? Didn't you use to work at Delightful Bites?"

She smiled. "Only for a few weeks. The early mornings killed me. Are you ready to order?"

"Do you mind if I ask a question first?"

The host sat someone in the booth behind us. Kelly's gaze shifted in that direction. "If it's quick. I got another table."

"Do you know Alex Danford?"

She tapped her pencil on her pad. "Chic Bohemian lady, long gray hair?"

"Yes. Do you remember her and a man arguing at Delightful Bites a few weeks ago?"

"Vaguely. He was all starch and clean lines, and she wore a painting smock and Birkenstock's. I was surprised they even knew each other. It got a little heated. I wasn't paying much attention. They got there so early I barely had time for a quick gulp of coffee. The only thing I remember was how red Ms. Danford was after he stormed out. She looked like she was going to cry and left before I could say anything to her." She shifted from foot to foot. "Are you ready to order?" We did.

I turned back to Rob. "So Alex was telling the truth. Or at least part of it. She said she was past Richard."

"Do you still care for Drew?"

"That's different. It seems like he goes out of his way to make my life miserable."

"Speaking of which, what's going on with Jenny?"

"It hasn't been pleasant. I love my daughter, and she's a smart girl, but she can't seem to understand why this is such a bad idea."

He touched my hand. "Likely the emotion of it all. And the chance to see London."

I groaned. "Patty said that too. I guess I'll have to try and swing a trip there either next year at spring break or next summer. This summer will be pretty crazy with college trips."

The food arrived. I cut into the tuna melt and took a bite. "This is delicious. It was the right choice. Nice and comforting. Speaking of which, I ran into your mother yesterday."

"I'm not sure how nice and comforting my mother is."

"She was in April and Sandy's new shop, C'est Magnifique."

"I'm covering their grand opening next week. I heard they're going to be serving champagne."

"Maybe I'll join you." I grinned.

"What did my mother have to say?"

"She was quite complimentary about the blouse I tried on. In fact, she bought it for me as a gift. You'll get to see it on Saturday when we go to the Greens' for dinner."

He caressed my hand. "I can't wait. You look good in everything."

"Flatterer. Have you heard anything more about Richard's case?"

"The police questioned both Mac and my mother. According to her, nothing new came up. They told Jay they were together all afternoon."

* * *

Rob came to the house early to pick me up for dinner at the Greens'. Jenny walked through the kitchen on her way out and barely acknowledged his presence. His eyebrow rose. "Not quite over it yet, is she?"

"How could you tell?" I put a cake into a carrier. "Ready to go?"

He picked up the bottle of wine and extended his hand to the cake carrier. "Want me to take that too?"

I surrendered it and locked the door behind me.

We pulled up to the Greens' house. My mouth dropped. The landscape was completely changed. A four-foot wrought-iron fence surrounded the yard. New trees and boxwoods had been planted, and water trickled somewhere nearby. "Diedra said she'd been gardening, but this is incredible. How did they get so much done since we picked them up for the church festival?"

Rob rang the doorbell. Kevin answered, took the wine and cake, and ushered us in. The living room still had lovely wood molding, but the look was far cozier due to the overstuffed sofas and vibrant art. I said, "This is lovely. You've done a nice job transforming the place. A client of mine used to live here."

"Thanks. We haven't changed that much inside. Most of our work has been outside."

He led us into the kitchen. Diedra was basting a chicken. Rob leaned over her shoulder. "That smells delicious."

She smiled. "It's the tarragon. It smells like licorice." She held up a discarded stem for Rob to smell.

"I can't wait."

"It'll be a little while yet. This needs to go back into the oven." She opened the stove and put the chicken back in. "I love your blouse, Merry."

"Thanks, Rob's mom gave it to me."

Diedra smiled. "How nice."

Kevin asked, "Is this a good time for the garden tour?"

"Perfect. Would anyone care for a drink? We'll have munchies to tide you over outside." Diedra added grapes to a tray with cheese and dried fruit.

I said, "Wine for me."

"Same," Rob echoed.

Kevin poured four glasses and handed them around. Diedra gave him the tray and pointed to the far corner of the garden. "Let's start by the pond."

I followed her lead. Bluestone pavers formed a meandering path leading past herb gardens and roses to an iris lined pond. Golden butterfly koi glimmered in the water. "I can't believe how much you've gotten done."

"We didn't do it all ourselves. We're getting too old for that. We had that nice young man who runs the local nursery bring his crew in."

"Why do you have a net over the pond?"

Kevin said, "To keep the herons out. In our last place, a heron ate a koi that was five years old. It was a golden koi like these, named Daisy."

Rob asked, "Do you have names for these yet?"

"The kids name them. They haven't been here since we put the fish in a week or so ago."

A small stream emerged into a trickling waterfall. It was peaceful. "Are those goldfish?" I motioned toward the fish peeking out from under a rock.

"Yes. They're shubunkins. See their calico pattern?"

"So pretty. And is that thyme between the pavers over there?"

"Wait until it gets going. It'll cover the stones if we're not careful. And it releases such a nice odor when walked on."

There was a small cocktail table with bistro chairs near the pond. Kevin extended his hand. "Let's sit here and talk."

We sat. He placed the nibbles on the table. I closed my eyes. "I could fall right asleep." I sat up abruptly. "Not that I'm bored. I'd find anything you have to say interesting."

Diedra's laugh tinkled. "If you're tired, go right ahead. We'll talk softly around you."

I smiled. "I don't think that's necessary."

"When I ran into you the other day, you seemed troubled. Is everything okay?"

"A disagreement with my ex. It's resolved now."

"I'm glad. This sleepy little town has had a lot going on lately. Such a terrible business with those men at the motel in town." Diedra shook her head. "You own the paper, Rob. Have you heard anything more about what happened?

"Detective Ziebold is still waiting on the coroner's report."

Kevin swirled his wine. "We heard they were shot. Shocking. I thought this was a safe town."

"It usually is."

Rob stood. "Do you mind if I take a closer look at your plants?"

Kevin said, "Not at all. Do you want company?"

"I won't be long. No need to get up." Rob wandered off.

I turned to Diedra. "Have you been to the new clothing shop in town yet? That's where Wanda got this blouse."

"I thought it wasn't opening until next week." She sipped her wine.

"They did a soft opening. But you're right; the grand opening is next week."

Kevin said, "Feel free to go without me."

I laughed. "Rob is going to cover it for the paper. I was thinking about going; Diedra, why don't you come with me." I leaned toward her. "He said they'd have champagne."

"Sign me up." She put cheese on a cracker.

I took a dried fig and bit into it. "These are good."

A timer rang from inside the house. Diedra rose. "Need to check on the chicken." She disappeared inside the kitchen.

Rob came back. "The rest of your garden is lovely. I like how you've incorporated tropicals with your perennials. Did I see a castor bean plant back there?" He pointed to the left. A fig caught in my throat, and I began to cough. Rob patted my back. "Are you okay Merry?

I gasped, "Water."

Kevin leaped up and hurried after Diedra.

I glared at Rob. "Why didn't you wait until we were alone?"

"I wanted to see his reaction, but I wasn't able to since his attention was focused on you."

Kevin came out of the back door. I coughed, and he handed me the water. I sipped it. "Thanks."

"Are you okay?" His brow furrowed.

I waved a hand since I was still drinking the water. "Fig went down the wrong way."

He turned to Rob. "I'm sorry. You asked me a question."

"I asked if that was a castor bean plant back there."

"Yes, it is. They have such pretty foliage, and the red plumes are lovely. Are you a fan?"

"They certainly seem to be popular around here."

Diedra called out. "Dinner's ready."

We wove our way through the kitchen to the dining room. She had a lovely, round wooden table that looked old. I ran my hand along it. "Is this wormy chestnut?"

Diedra beamed. "It is. Family heirloom." Her smile dimmed. "I always thought my daughter would inherit it. Now that she's gone, I guess it will go to one of my sons."

Kevin touched Diedra's hand. She winced. "It's been a number of years, but it still seems so fresh. I can't believe that wretched man took them from us."

"What man?" Rob asked.

"The one who was married to your mother. Richard Franco. We couldn't prove anything. But we knew he was behind it. Those men who were killed at the motel used to work for him. They had the nerve to come to our house and ask us questions about where we had been the day Richard died. I couldn't believe they were standing at my door." She shuddered. "They probably were the ones who cut the brakes to our daughter's car." Her hand trembled as she reached for the wine.

I said, "It must have been so difficult for you."

"It still is. I hope you never feel the pain of losing a child."

I crossed myself.

* * *

Rob took his time driving home. I curled against the passenger door. "It must be incredibly hard to know who was responsible for your daughter's death and not be able to prove it. That man was scum."

The signal clicked as he turned into my driveway. "I didn't care very much for Richard when he was alive. Now that he's dead, I can't stand him. He caused so much heartache."

I climbed out of the car. "Agreed. But no one should have killed him. Two wrongs don't make a right."

Rob opened my back door. "I wish we could have brought your cake back. It was so good. I loved the peach layer, and you know that I'm a fan of cream frostings."

"It's better it stayed with them. I don't need the calories."

He rummaged in the pantry. "Any cookies?"

"Didn't you get enough to eat?"

"I did. That chicken was amazing. I'm glad Diedra said she'd email me the recipe." He grabbed the cookie jar. "Mind?"

I shook my head. "Have at it. Milk, coffee, or after-dinner drink?"

"Bailey's and chocolate chip cookies sound like a match made in heaven."

I retrieved the liqueur and cordial glasses and handed them to him. He poured two, picked them up, and wandered into the living room. I trailed him. "They seem like such a lovely couple."

"They do. Too bad they sought revenge against Richard." He sank onto the sofa and unscrewed the cookie jar lid.

"How do you know it was them?"

"Go through your list."

I opened the end table drawer and pulled out my pad. I flipped it to the correct page. "Your mom."

"Non-starter."

I shrugged. "The Greens"

"Highly likely."

"Alex."

"Mysterious."

I tucked my feet under me and leaned against Rob's shoulder. "One more scenario."

His left eyebrow lifted.

"Your new father-in-law Mac together with your mother. It's convenient that he and your mother hooked up on vacation and then rekindled their romance when she and her husband came to visit you."

Rob sipped his drink. "Three to four people. All with good motives. But who did it?"

"I think it's time we chatted with the good Detective to see if he's found out anything new."

I tipped my face toward Rob's. He gave me a lingering kiss. I withdrew and put my finger on his lips. "Tomorrow." I kissed him. "Yum. You taste like Bailey's."

"Is Jenny home?"

"She's out with Jacob. I lifted my eyes to the clock. Should be home any minute now."

"Darn."

* * *

Sirens blared early the next morning. Still half asleep, I put the pillow over my ear. My room swam with flashing lights. I sat straight up in bed, and then I rushed to the bathroom window. The emergency squad was next door at Alex's. I pulled on sweats and a t-shirt and ran downstairs. They wheeled Alex into the ambulance, her face covered by an oxygen mask. Ed stood nearby, and I ran to him. "What happened?"

He rubbed his eyes. "I'm not sure. I was up early and happened to glance out the window. Alex saw me and waved. She was painting. I was mesmerized by her sure brushstrokes. The next thing I knew, she fell over. I called 911 as I was running out the back door."

We walked to where her easel stood. A partly eaten muffin lay in the grass. I picked it up and sniffed. "This smells like peanuts."

The ambulance roared away. I stared after it. "Who would have given Alex something like that?"

Andy came running across the alley. "What happened?"

"Someone gave Alex peanuts. I'll call Jay."

I carried the remains of the muffin into my kitchen. Andy and Ed followed. I put it into a baggie and picked up my phone. Jay picked up on the first ring. "What?"

"Someone tried to kill my neighbor."

He sighed. "I'll be right over."

I put the coffee on, and it was ready by the time Jay arrived. He walked in the back door and Andy, Ed, and I started talking over each other.

Jay held up his hand. "Coffee first. Then one at a time."

I poured the coffee, and Ed told Jay what he had seen. Then I handed Jay the baggie. "We found this near where Alex collapsed."

He took it from me. "Thanks. I have to stop at the station first, and then I'll go to the hospital. Not a word to anyone until I get back. It could be that someone just made a mistake." He left.

I put his mug in the dishwasher and then wiped the counter. Ed stood abruptly. "We should go to the hospital. She's all alone. Merry, you get ready. I'll bring the car around in ten minutes."

I ran up the stairs, pulled a brush through my hair, and splashed my face with water. A quick toothbrush and mouthwash swish, and I walked out of my bedroom. Jenny's door opened. "What's all the commotion?"

Ed's car pulled into the driveway. I ran down the stairs. "Can't talk now. Something happened to Alex. I'll text you from the hospital." I grabbed my purse and slammed the door behind me. Andy waved for me to hurry up, and Ed barely waited for me to hop in the backseat before backing out. "Let's get there in one piece, shall we?"

Ed's eyes met mine in the rearview mirror. He mouthed. "Sorry," as he sped to the hospital.

The nurse led us to Alex's room. "The rules are only two visitors at a time."

Andy flashed his dimples at her. "We won't tell if you don't."

She opened the door. "Fifteen minutes max."

Alex was sitting up in bed, and her color had returned. She was nibbling a saltine and drinking ginger ale.

I hurried to her side. "How are you feeling?"

She flinched. "Better than I should. If Ed hadn't rushed over, I don't know what would have happened." She turned to me. "I only ate it because you baked it, and you're aware of my allergy. I'm usually so careful."

My eyes widened, and I stepped back. "What do you mean? I didn't give you anything."

"The muffins were on my back stoop this morning on one of your kitchen plates. And there was a note from you. I thought you baked them to apologize for doubting the story I told about Richard and me. They looked like the Morning Glory muffins you make. Only these had peanuts in them." She sneezed. "If it hadn't been for this stupid cold, I would have smelled it."

"I didn't leave you muffins."

"Who else would have? And who would have known I was mad at you?"

Detective Ziebold walked through the door. He stopped just inside the door. "You'll have to leave; I need to question Ms. Danford."

No one moved.

"What's wrong?"

"Alex said that I left her the muffins. But I...I didn't."

"Wait for me outside."

We shuffled past him. I stopped. "I didn't do it."

"Outside." He shut the door after me.

I paced the corridor. "How could Alex think I would give her peanuts? I would never do something like that. I'm so careful. I knew she was allergic."

Andy guided me to a chair. "You're making me nervous. Ed, could you see if they have any tea here?" Ed walked toward the cafeteria.

I sat. "Did you see a note? Or a plate?"

"All I saw was you putting the muffin in a baggy."

"We should get back there. I want to check out her backyard." I got to my feet.

Andy pulled me back down. "We're not going anywhere. Detective Ziebold told us to wait here."

I groaned and put my head in my hands.

A few minutes later, Ed returned with the tea. He handed me a cup.

I took a sip and almost spat it out. "How much sugar did you put in this?"

"Two packets. I figured you had a shock and needed the lift."

"I only use a little. Thanks for the tea, but I'll pass."

He handed me his. "Here. Drink this. It's black."

I sipped. "Much better. Thanks. Anyway, I was trying to convince Andy to drive me home. I want to check out Alex's backyard."

Andy rolled his eyes. "I told her we were waiting for the Detective."

Ed sank onto the chair on the other side of me. "And that's what we are going to do."

A few minutes later, Jay walked out of Alex's room. He motioned for Ed to slide over. Ed moved to the next chair and Jay took his place. "Merry, did you make those muffins?"

"No. I didn't."

"She said there was a note from you and the muffins were on your plate."

I frowned. "I don't know how they got on my plate. Maybe it wasn't my plate. Maybe it only looked like the plates I have."

Jay stood. "Merry, come with me. I want to go back to Alex's house. Depending on what we find, I may have questions for you."

I stood and walked behind him out the door.

Andy ran after me. "We're going to find out when Alex will be released. I'll call you later."

Jay waved me forward. I nodded at Andy and joined Jay in his car. "Do you want me in the back seat?"

He held the front door for me. "I haven't arrested you. Yet."

I slid in.

He circled the car and got into the driver's seat. "Explain to me exactly what happened this morning. Don't leave anything out."

I detailed the morning from my perspective. He turned into my driveway. I jumped out and ran to the back of Alex's house. Jay yelled after me, "Don't touch anything." I slowed my pace, allowing him to catch up. We approached her back steps. A white plate etched with green ivy sat on the top one. It held three muffins.

I leaned over, being careful not to touch it. "It does look like one of my plates."

He bagged the plate and its contents. "I'd like one of yours for comparison."

"Fine." I grimaced.

"She said there was a note from you."

"I didn't write it or bring over the muffins."

He sighed. "Let's look for the note."

We scanned near the back steps and then spread out to the backyard. No note. I turned toward the house. "Maybe she took it inside?"

He put out his hand to stop me. "I'll look."

I scanned my driveway to see if it had blown there. Nothing. Then I walked back to the alleyway; it was clear. The door shut. I hurried back to Jay. "Anything?"

"No. I'll talk to her later and see if she put it somewhere."

"I'll get you one of my plates." I led the way back to my house. When I opened the back door, Jenny was sitting at the counter.

"What happened? You said you text me, but you didn't."

"Not now."

Jay walked in behind me. I felt Jenny's eyes follow me as I retrieved one of the plates and handed it to him. He examined it. "Looks the same."

I did a quick count. "I'm missing a few."

"Let's go down to the station, and you can make a formal statement."

Jenny's eyes widened. "What happened? Why do you have to go to the station?"

Jay held the door for me. I walked out. "Call Rob. Tell him I need a lawyer."

CHAPTER 19

They questioned me for two hours. I couldn't believe it took so long to go over such a simple story. I had been at the Greens' for dinner the night before, Rob had been at my house until midnight, and the sirens had woken me in time to see Alex being loaded into the ambulance. How on earth did they think I had time to bake muffins! If only they could find the note. Then I could prove it wasn't me. Finally, my lawyer and I were able to leave.

Rob waited for us by the front desk. "Jay can't think you did this."

I collapsed into his arms. "It was my plate. Or at least I think it was. How could someone have gotten my plate?"

Rob rubbed my back. "Merry, you're always baking things for people. Someone might not have returned it, and you didn't notice."

I backed away. "I always put masking tape on the bottom with my name on it so people can return it!" I walked back to the interview room and knocked.

Jay answered the door. "What?"

"Was there masking tape on the bottom of the plate?"

"I didn't see any." He walked past me to his office. He returned. "No tape."

My lawyer held up her hand. "The person could have washed it, and the tape came off. Or the person could have taken the tape from the plate."

Jay walked back into the interview room and closed the door.

Rob asked my lawyer, "What's next?"

"They haven't charged her with anything. Hopefully, this whole mess will be straightened out soon, and nothing else will happen." Her finger rose. "Merry, listen to me very carefully. Stay away from Alex."

"But she was in the hospital. She's probably still weak. I should bring her chicken soup."

Rob's mouth dropped. "Listen to what you're saying."

I rubbed my forehead. "Okay. No contact. And definitely no food."

Rob put his arm around me, and we left the police station. My phone dinged with a text from Patty: "Heard you were in the slammer."

I groaned. Monday was going to be fun.

✳ ✳ ✳

Cheryl was waiting for me by the door Monday morning. "Going to be busy, boss. Half the town wants to know why you tried to kill Alex."

"I didn't try to kill her."

"I know. I can't imagine you poisoning anyone."

I led the way to my office. "How many calls have we gotten?"

"A few. We're handling them."

"What a nightmare."

"Andy wanted to know if you could stop by the shop at one for lunch.

"Let him know I'll be there."

✳ ✳ ✳

I strode up the street to Andy and Ed's antique shop and café, Tempting Treasures and Tasty Treats. Andy wasn't quite ready, so I wandered through his shop. He had a new mahogany Chippendale dresser that I couldn't help but drool over. I checked the price. *Nope.*

"Ready?" Andy touched my shoulder.

"Starving."

"You're going to want to have today's special. Swedish meatballs on toast points. It comes with a side salad."

"Sold."

He told the waiter, and we headed outside. The intimate patio held eight tables, which were shaded by the building. Overflowing planters stuffed with scarlet petunia wave hung from the wrought-iron fencing. "It's so nice that you decided to be open on Mondays in the spring and summer."

He sat back. "It's more work, but we have better staff now. We feel like we can take time off, or have lunch with a friend."

"I can't help but think you had a reason for this one."

"I'm crushed that you'd think I had an ulterior motive."

I sipped my iced tea and waited.

"Okay. Yes, I did. I wanted to talk about what happened yesterday. Detective Ziebold was pretty quick to take you back to Alex's house. And then I heard you went to the station."

I groaned. "First you need to tell me about Alex. Is she okay?"

"She's fine. They released her in the early afternoon, and she was out painting again this morning, so I guess no harm done."

I frowned. "They think I tried to hurt her. What did she say about the note?"

"She doesn't know where it went. She said it was on the top of the saran wrapped dish and that it must have blown away when she took one of the muffins out."

"How was the note attached?"

"I don't know. Tape?"

"Didn't you ask her?"

"I'm sure the police did."

Our lunches arrived. The meatballs, mushrooms, and luscious sauce were what I needed. "This is so good."

Andy winked. "I'll be sure to let the chef know you liked it. Now spill. What happened to you?"

I told him about the plate.

"You're always baking stuff. Ed and I have two of your plates in our house right now."

"I guess that's why I'm missing a few."

"I'll bring them by this week."

"No rush." The salad was lovely too. Ed had laced butter lettuce with radicchio, and its bitter taste was the perfect foil for the creamy sauce of the meatballs. "Are you going to the C'est Magnifique grand opening Wednesday?"

"Yes. Ed is catering, and we're letting them borrow our patio. Plus Ed's mother's birthday is coming up, and I still need to get her a gift."

"They have lovely things. Wanda bought me the nicest blouse."

He laughed.

"What?"

"It's not funny, but you and Wanda are both suspects. Maybe you have more in common than you thought."

* * *

Wednesday morning, I bent over the freezer to see what Jenny could have for supper. There was leftover chicken and rice. I pulled out the packet and left it in the fridge. Half-way through writing a note, Jenny appeared. She kissed me on the cheek. I stepped backward, jaw-dropping. "That's a surprise."

"I decided you were right. We can go to London next year."

My eyebrow rose. "That's very grown-up of you."

She smiled. "I know. Are you going to the grand opening tonight?"

"Yes. There are leftovers in the fridge."

"Thanks. What time will you be home?"

"Rob and I will probably go out afterward, but I should be home by ten."

"Have fun." She disappeared up the stairs.

That was weird. As much as I loved my daughter, she definitely took longer than that to get over one of her snits. She didn't talk to me for a month after I wouldn't let her go hang gliding. Maybe she was getting older. I shrugged and walked out the door.

Late that day, I picked up Diedra and chauffeured her to the grand opening. Balloons hung from the sign, and the store window was a delight. Mannequins were artfully arrayed in spring clothes and what looked like real flowers punctuated the display. Diedra grinned. "This is going to be fun."

The store was packed with people, and I lost sight of Diedra for a minute. She was examining the multi-colored scarves. I caught her eye and motioned toward the back door. "Let's get champagne and then we can come back to the shop." I strode down the two back steps and up one to Ed's patio. A makeshift bar had been set up, and waiters wove through the crowd with glasses of champagne. I snagged two and handed one to Diedra.

"Thanks. It's crowded here, isn't it?"

"It is. I hope it translates into business for April and Sandy. Look, there's Rob." I pointed.

Rob was taking photos of the crowd. Between the overflowing planter boxes and fairy lights twinkling, it looked magical. A waiter stopped by with cheddar cheese puffs. I took one and told Diedra, "These are wonderful; you'll be sorry if you miss out."

She ate one, and her eyes closed. "That is so good. I'm glad he walked away, I think I might have stolen the tray from him."

A woman almost tripped on my foot. "Merry. Thank goodness. I meant to stop by."

I gasped. "Alex. I'm supposed to stay away from you."

"Poppycock. You just put nuts in by mistake. You didn't do it on purpose."

"I didn't bake those muffins. You have to believe me."

She touched my arm. "I believe you, but if it wasn't a mistake, who gave them to me? And why did they leave a note from you? Do you think they'd try again?" Her gaze skittered. "I think I'll go home now." She wove through the tables to the door.

Rob hurried to my side. "Are you okay?"

I stared at Alex's back. "I wasn't trying to worry her. I just wanted her to know it wasn't me. I'm fine. Continue taking your pictures." He frowned but moved on.

Diedra said, "What happened? I feel like I missed a chapter."

People rose from one of the tables near us. I claimed a chair and held one out for Diedra. I sat and explained.

"That doesn't sound good. How would the person have gotten your plate?"

I hung my head. "Who knows? And they still haven't found the note."

Diedra raised her champagne glass. "This too shall pass. It's what I always tell my kids." She teared up. "And usually it's true."

"I'm sorry. This seems trivial compared to what you've been through."

"What happened to Alex could have been much worse. And anyway, what we prayed for happened."

"What was that?"

"For that man to die."

My mouth dropped. "You prayed for Richard's death?"

"Every day." She flinched. "I know it's bad of me, but I just couldn't help it."

"What about his associates."

"Them too." She coughed.

Rob returned. "I think I have enough photos, time for a glass of champagne." He motioned to a waiter, who was passing out glasses. "Anyone else need one?" Deidra raised her hand. He took two glasses and handed her one.

Diedra rose. "I think I'll take a stroll and see what the store has."

I said, "I'll join you in a minute."

"Take your time." She wandered into the shop, champagne glass in hand.

Rob sat in her seat. "You look pale."

"She said she prayed every day for Richard's death. Maybe she and her husband figured that prayers weren't enough and decided to do something about it."

* * *

We dropped Diedra off. Rob tried to talk me into going out for dinner, but I had had enough of people for one day. I strode through the back door. "Jenny, we're home!"

A door slammed, and she ran down the stairs. "I thought you were going out."

"We decided not to. Rob's making omelets. Want one?"

"No, I had the leftovers. Thanks."

"Is that the washing machine running?"

"Yes. Did you need it?"

"No. Just wondered. You don't normally do the wash."

Jenny said, "I'll be upstairs if you need me. I've got the timer set, so don't worry about moving the clothes to the dryer, I'll handle it." She dashed out of the kitchen.

Rob laid bacon, eggs, spring onions, and broccoli on the counter. "Do I sense a thaw?"

"You do. An amazing turnaround that started this morning. And now she's doing the wash. Wonders will never cease."

The bacon sizzled in the pan. He chopped the broccoli and added it. "Cheese?"

"Yes, I have Swiss." I took it from the fridge.

There was a rap at the back door. Andy walked in. "Am I intruding?"

"Never. Want a glass of wine or omelet?"

"Can't stay. Ed's making shrimp stir fry at home. How he's in the mood to cook after catering a party, I'll never know. But since I'm the beneficiary, I'm not going to complain." He handed me a plate. "I thought we had two, but it turns out it was one." He bounded out the door.

CHAPTER 20

Thursday's work started outside the office. I visited homes and businesses to make sure that the outstanding claims from the storm had been settled and that the work had been completed. Not all agents do this, but I found it helped create stronger bonds. Several customers asked me about Alex; I reassured them I hadn't baked the muffins, and they seemed to believe me.

My stomach growled. I checked my phone. If I hoofed it, I could have lunch at home and then go to the office. Another rumble and the decision was made. As I drove down my street, Jacob shut his trunk, got in the car, and pulled away from the curb, and I took the spot he vacated.

I ran up the steps and let myself in the front door. Jenny sprawled on the couch, phone in hand. She sat up. "Hi, Mom. I didn't expect you home this early."

"Lunch. What was Jacob doing here?"

"He stopped by to drop off an old game I wanted to try." Her foot tapped.

My gaze wandered about the room. "Where is it?"

"What?" Her foot moved faster.

"The game he dropped off."

"Oh. I took it up to my room." She stood. "If that's the end of twenty questions, I'll see you later. I had lunch already." Her ponytail bobbed as she ran up the stairs.

Something wasn't ringing true. I passed my office door on the way to the kitchen. It was open. *Strange.* I walked in and did a quick scan.

Nothing seemed to be out of place. I shrugged, shut the door behind me, and wandered into the kitchen. Leftover tuna salad or chicken breast? The tuna won. I made a sandwich, poured myself a glass of milk, and sat at the counter.

I took a bite and then pulled over a pad I keep near the phone. Clicking the pen, I started a list of people who might have wanted to harm Alex. It was a short list, headed by the generic "people from before she moved here" to the Greens. I began to doodle. There wasn't more I could add to the first group, as I didn't know who she knew before. The Greens. Hmm. Richard had been married to Alex when he killed the Greens' daughter. Maybe they blamed her. Perhaps they thought that she could have stopped it somehow. I shuddered. Maybe they were going to target all of Richard's wives. That would put Rob's mother, Wanda, on their radar.

I finished my sandwich and loaded the dishwasher. Walking out the door, I texted Rob: "Dinner tonight? My house at six?"

"I'll be there."

The afternoon was full of spreadsheets, and I was eager to leave at the end of the day. I hurried home. As I passed Alex's house, I thought I saw her peering out. The curtain swung shut.

My shoulders slumped as I trudged into the kitchen. Alex must be worried, and she's over there all by herself. Maybe I should have Andy run over and check on her.

The chicken had defrosted in the refrigerator. I cubed it and then made a quick soy marinade. It went back into the fridge, and I poured myself a glass of wine. I sat on the window seat and admired the garden. Alex walked out her door and jumped when Rob's car pulled in the drive. She rushed back inside.

Rob gave a quick knock and strode through the back door. I greeted him with a kiss. "The strangest thing just happened."

His eyebrow rose.

"Alex walked out, but when she saw you, she turned tail and went back in."

"Maybe she forgot something."

"Maybe she didn't want you to see her doing whatever she was about to do."

He poured himself a glass of wine. "Or maybe she's worried that someone's going to try again."

I shuddered. "I want all this to be over with."

"It has been busy lately."

"Let's sit out back. I'm doing a stir fry, so dinner shouldn't take long."

He held the door for me. "What's new?"

I sat. "It looks like all the storm claims have been handled, so things should calm down at work."

"That's good news."

"It is. And now for troubling news."

"What happened?"

"Nothing happened. Or at least I hope nothing's happening. Jacob pulled away from the curb when I came home for lunch today."

"So?"

"What was he doing here? Jenny knows I don't like her to have boys over when I'm not home."

He reached for my hand. "What did she say when you asked her about it?"

"She said he dropped off a game. I would have felt better if I'd seen it."

His eyebrow rose.

"And my office door was open. I always keep it shut."

"I'm confused. Were you worried they were fooling around or were you worried they were in your office?"

"Both, I guess."

"What would they want in your office?"

"I have no idea." I studied the flowering Jackmanii clematis by the fence. Such pretty purple flowers. Was that a white flower?

Rob snapped his fingers. "We were talking about Jenny and Jacob. What are you looking at?"

"That clematis has purple flowers."

He turned toward the fence. "It does."

"What's that three-quarters of the way up? It's white; how would my purple clematis start blooming white? Maybe it's a mutation."

Rob walked to the trellis. After a moment he said, "Would you get me a tweezer and a plastic bag?"

I leaped up. "It's not a flower. It's a piece of paper. Is it the note?"

"I don't know."

"I'll be right back." I grabbed the tweezers from the downstairs powder room and baggie from the kitchen. I ran out and handed him the tweezers.

He teased the paper from the clematis. "It must have blown here from next door."

I opened the baggie, and he dropped the note inside. I sealed it and then held up the baggie. "Rob, it looks like my handwriting."

"Let's take it inside."

I trailed behind him. "Maybe it's not the note. Maybe it's something else."

He carefully flattened the piece of paper through the baggie. It read: "Hope you enjoy the muffins, Merry."

I sank onto the kitchen stool. "It's my handwriting. And it references muffins." I grabbed the antacids. "How?"

Rob rubbed my back. "We're going to have to give it to Jay."

My mouth dropped. "But then he'll think I did it."

He stared at me.

"You're right. Momentary lapse. I'll call him." I made the call and then sat there, stunned. Rob continued to examine the note.

Fifteen minutes later, Jay walked through the back door. "Where's the note?"

Rob pointed to the counter.

Jay whistled. "Merry, you told me you hadn't written this. I'm no handwriting expert, but it looks like yours."

My head drooped. "It is. I don't know why it is, but it is."

"There's something odd here," Rob said.

Jay leaned over the counter. "What."

"See how the bottom edges of the paper are scalloped?"

Jay nodded.

"Now look at the top. It's a straight edge. It's almost like someone cut something off."

I rushed over. "Show me."

He traced the border.

"I'll get a blank sheet so we can compare it." I went into my office, retrieved it, and walked back to the counter. I laid it down next to the one Rob had pulled from the clematis. "You're right. And the one from the trellis doesn't have my header." The blank sheet had Meredith March emblazoned across the top.

"Someone is trying to frame Merry." Rob tapped the notepaper with the pencil.

* * *

Jenny seemed almost manic at dinner. She insisted on cleaning up afterward and encouraged Rob and me to have an after-dinner drink in the living room. We complied.

I curled up against Rob on the couch. "Tell me that's not weird behavior."

"Maybe she recognizes she was wrong, and she's trying to make it up to you."

"Perhaps, but I know my daughter, and I can't help but think something is going on." I sighed. "With someone trying to frame me, your mother accused of murder, and Alex's hospital visit, everything seems to be topsy-turvy.

I was tired, so we had an early evening. I stopped by Jenny's room on my way to bed and rapped softly. I walked in and sat on the bed. "Wow. It looks so clean in here."

"Thanks. I thought it needed it."

"Is there anything you want to tell me?"

She chewed her bottom lip. "Everything's fine. I'm sorry I was such a pain."

I hugged her. "I love you. You know you can tell me anything, right?"

"I know." She hugged me back. "Jacob and I are going to dinner early tomorrow and a movie after, so I won't be here when you get home from work."

"Got it." I rose and went out the door.

"I love you, Mom."

I blew her a kiss and shut the door behind me. *Maybe she is growing up.*

* * *

Friday was crazy, and Rob arrived promptly at six to take me to dinner. We decided on a quick one at the Golden Skillet. I was tired, and all I could think of was taking a long soak in the tub and diving into my book. He dropped me at the house with a lingering kiss and embrace.

I trudged up the stairs and ran the bath. Feeling the need for some pampering, I added the lavender bath salts Patty had given me. After swirling the water a few times, I climbed in. My back slid down to a comfortable recline, and I wet the washcloth and draped it over my face—finally the me time I needed. As I tried to relax, something kept nagging at me just out of reach. Why had Jenny been so nice lately? And why had she seemed so nervous last night? And why was her room so clean?

I jumped out of the tub, wrapped a towel around me, and ran down the stairs into my office. I bent over the safe, turned the dial, and opened it. I yanked out the red file. One passport. Mine.

I ran to the phone. Thank goodness I had photocopied the ticket Drew sent. I reached an automated recording and punched in the flight number. "Flight 4099 departed on time to London at five o'clock."

I fell into the chair. She went to London to meet Drew.

* * *

I texted Rob and then ran upstairs to change. It seemed like he arrived within minutes of the text. I paced the kitchen. "I knew something was off. If I hadn't been so distracted with Alex, I would have figured it out sooner." I kicked one of the chairs. "I can't believe she lied to me. I'm going to kill her."

Rob held out a chair. "Merry, sit. You're beet red. Having a heart attack won't solve anything."

"I can't sit. I need to book a ticket on the next flight to London."

"You don't even know where they are staying."

I glared at him. "If that kid ever wants to come back here, she better answer the flaming text I sent."

He opened my iPad. "All right, but I'm going with you."

There was a knock at the door, and Jay walked in. "Meredith March, I'm arresting you for the attempted murder of Alex Danford."

CHAPTER 21

The cot in the county jail was murder on my back. The décor was that special kind of prison gray, and the bathroom was quite public. I paced the cell, and mid-morning my lawyer sprung me. She cautioned, "I got them to set bail; promise me you'll stay away from Ms. Danford."

"You don't need to worry about that; I'm catching the next flight to London."

"No, you're not."

"My daughter is on her own, and she was supposed to have landed there—" I checked my watch—"early this morning. Trust me; I'm getting on a plane."

"Merry, you had to surrender your passport as a condition of making bail."

I felt faint. "What am I going to do?" I turned on my heel, walked out the courthouse door, and into the police station next door. I knocked at Jay's door.

"Come in."

I opened the door and strode to his desk. "Jay, you know I didn't do this."

"Merry, if it had been up to me, I wouldn't have charged you. The new District Attorney is trying to make a name for himself."

I sank into a chair. "It's the absolute worst time for this. Jenny flew to London. She's meeting Drew there."

His eyes widened. "Ex-husband Drew? The one the FBI is looking for?"

"The only ex I have."

"Where is he staying in London?"

My phone binged. Jenny's text read: "Know you're mad but had to do this. Can reach me by phone. Address follows."

I handed the phone to Jay. "At least she told me where she was."

He made a note of the address. "I'm sorry, Merry. I know it's difficult, but there is nothing I can do now."

There was a knock at the door.

"Come."

Rob rushed in. "I have a ticket. My flight leaves in three hours." He stood over Jay. "You're not detaining her, are you? I need a ride to the airport."

"No. She's free to go, and you are too."

I tore out of the station. Rob raced after me. "Merry, wait up."

"How is this happening?"

He wrapped me in his arms. "I'll bring her back safe and sound. Trust me."

"What kind of mother am I?" I mumbled into his chest.

"The best. And now we need to go if I'm going to make my plane. I'll drive to the airport, and you can bring the car back."

As I brooded in the passenger seat, the ride to the airport seemed to take forever. Rob pulled up to the curb and jumped out. He grabbed his carry-on from the trunk, came to my door, and pulled it open. "Merry, you can't sit here. It's busy."

I got out and kissed him. "Thanks for doing this."

He accompanied me to the driver's side and held the door as I got in. "I'll bring her back. I promise." He bent for another kiss and then was gone, jogging toward the terminal.

My head sank to the steering wheel. I tried deep breathing but was interrupted by a tap on the window. A policeman said, "You'll have to move along. Are you okay?"

I gave him a weak smile and started the car. Somehow I made it home. I pulled Rob's car into the drive, behind a silver Mercedes convertible. *Who on earth?* I strode to the front door and opened it.

Wanda was on the sofa. "Your back door was open. Where have you been? I've been trying to reach Rob, and all I get is voicemail."

I collapsed onto one of the chairs. "He got on a plane. He's going to London."

"London? We were supposed to go to dinner."

"It was a last-minute thing. It's a long story, actually, and I don't feel up to telling it right now."

"Mac thought I was going to dinner with Rob, so he made other plans." She examined her manicure. "I wouldn't say no to a glass of wine."

I suppressed a groan. "White?"

"Of course. And maybe some of that cheese you used to have. The Swiss." She stood. "It's lovely outside."

She didn't wait to help carry anything. She eased out the back door, and the cats made a break for it. I grimaced, retrieved a bottle of white, and poured two glasses. The block of Swiss was soon cut into smaller pieces and deposited on a plate. Then I put everything on a tray and opened the back door. I walked out and came to a dead stop.

Diedra was sitting next to Wanda. "Hello, Merry. You've been so kind to us, taking us to the fete, and introducing me around, so I baked carrot cupcakes to thank you." She stood and handed me the carrier. "The frosting's cream cheese so you probably want to get that into the refrigerator."

I lifted it. "They look amazing, thanks. Would you care for a glass of wine?"

She nodded. "If it's not too much trouble."

I handed her a glass and took the cupcakes into the house. Then I retrieved a folding chair from the shed, brushed it off, and sat down. "Wanda, you should see the garden the Greens put in. It's beautiful."

Wanda examined her nails. "I'm not a gardener. We have a team that keeps everything looking good. I suppose you and Kevin have to do all the work."

"We hired someone to do the heavy lifting, but we enjoy being outdoors and tending to the plants."

Wanda gave a slight cough. "This is fascinating, but I'm late for an appointment."

"Your dead husband even complimented us on it. Not that we needed any compliments from him." She shuddered.

Wanda started. "When was Richard there?"

"Just before he died. He wanted to make sure we weren't going to make trouble for him in town."

I leaned forward. "What day was that?"

"The day he died. He threatened us." Diedra shook her head. "Odious man."

Wanda looked down her nose. "You are referring to my husband."

"If rumor is to be believed, you were remarried after an unseemly short time, so I have no idea why you'd defend him."

I shook my head. "I'm sorry. I'm a little fuzzy. Did you say you saw Richard the day he died?"

She stood. "If I were you, Merry, I'd stop asking so many questions. Some rocks aren't meant to be turned over." She strolled out the back gate.

I took two pieces of cheese, threw them into my mouth, and then mumbled, "So the Greens saw Richard the day he died."

Wanda rose to her feet. "I find I'm not in the mood for this, after all. Would you have my son call me when he has a chance?" She put her wine glass on the table and left.

I ran after her to close the gate so the cats couldn't escape. A moment later, Wanda reappeared. "Rob's car is blocking mine. You'll have to move it."

I took my time, strolled to the kitchen for the keys, and wandered past the Mercedes.

Wanda's fingers tapped on the dash. "Could you move any slower?"

"Potentially." And then under my breath, "But then you'd still be here." I waved and backed out of the drive. Her car shot out, and she didn't give me another glance.

I parked the car, locked it, and went through the house to the backyard. Courvoisier and Bailey were on the table, munching the cheese. "Bad cats." I put the plate into the kitchen, returned to the backyard, and plopped onto the chair. The glass of wine was halfway to my lips when Patty opened the gate.

She sat next to me. "Looks like you've been having a party."

"Diedra and Wanda."

"Those are some strange bedfellows. I'll take this used glass inside and get a clean one." She went into the kitchen and came back out brandishing the new glass. "I hear you've been in the slammer. What was it like?"

I stared straight ahead. "You have no idea."

She put her hand out and turned my face toward hers. "I think you better tell me everything."

I did.

"So Jenny's in London, Rob's en route to retrieve her, and Diedra saw Richard the day he died."

"But who poisoned Alex and shot Scarface and Big Ears. And who's trying to frame me?"

"It's suspicious that someone cut the top off the note. You said it was in your handwriting. When would you have written it?"

My brow furrowed. "I brought Alex Morning Glory muffins when she first moved here. But the note said something like 'Welcome to the Neighborhood,' and the next line was 'Hope you enjoy the muffins.'"

"Someone cut off the top of the note and left the second part."

My eyes widened. "Who would do that? And how would someone have gotten the note?"

She petted Courvoisier. "I don't know." She checked her watch. "Oops. I need to get moving. I promised Patrick I'd take the kids bowling tonight. Do you want to come?"

"Thanks, but no. I have a lot to think about."

"Should I come back later?"

"I'm afraid I wouldn't be good company. I'm in dire need of a shower and some heavy-duty teeth brushing. Plus as much as I adore you, I think I'd rather be alone."

Patty kissed the top of my head. "Try not to worry too much." She walked out the gate.

I gathered the glasses, made my way into the kitchen, and lured the cats inside by a promise of treats. I glanced at my phone. Nothing. Rob wouldn't be landing for another two hours. I wandered into the living room and picked up my book.

The second time I reread the third paragraph, I put the book down. *Maybe some warm milk.*

I slid the mug into the microwave, pressed start, and paced the floor. After two minutes, it was done. I took the cup and sat on the window seat. The clock chimed ten.

Unable to sit still, I walked back into the living room. It was going to be a long night. I finally went upstairs to Jenny's room and laid down on her bed. Her room looked unnaturally clean. I wanted to take some of her clothes out of the closet and leave them on the back of her chair and window seat. I resisted and turned on my side. Her pillow smelled like her shampoo, slightly floral and fresh. Tears filled my eyes. I sat up and blew my nose. Getting upset wasn't going to solve anything. My phone dinged with a text from Rob: "Landed. Will call from hotel."

He didn't have any baggage, so hopefully, he'd get through customs quickly. It was nearly four in the morning in London. Even though I wanted him to get to Jenny quickly, it'd probably be best if he got a few hours of sleep. If he could. I sighed. I certainly wouldn't be able to.

I paced the floor of Jenny's room. It was too cramped, so I moved into the hallway. I walked from the guest bedroom to the wall in my bedroom and back. At least I'd get my steps in. Maybe it was time to redo the guest bedroom; the plaid curtains looked dated. My phone rang. I stabbed the answer button. "Rob?"

"Got to the hotel. I plan to head over to Drew's at eight."

"Maybe you should go now."

"Merry, any way you look at it, this is not likely to go well. It'll be worse if I wake everyone up. I booked Jenny and me on a flight out later today. I'll make sure she's on it. Try to get some sleep."

"The waiting is making me crazy."

"Hang in there. I'm going to try and get a few hours of sleep. I love you."

"Love you too. Thanks for doing this." I hung up.

I walked into my bathroom and eyed the sleeping pills. Nope. Just in case the phone rings. Going to have to tough it out.

CHAPTER 22

It felt like a dump truck of sand emptied into my eyes during the few seconds of hard-fought sleep I must have gotten. I pulled my phone from under my pillow. Nothing. I texted: "What's going on?" to Rob. No response. I padded into the bathroom and squirted Visine into my eyes. A little better, but not much. I brushed my teeth, donned a t-shirt and shorts, and sleepwalked my way downstairs.

Somehow the coffee machine button got pushed and the cats fed. I passed the window. The birdbath was empty. Darn. I forgot to fill it last night. I stumbled out the back door, turned the hose on, and filled it. Rubbing my face, I wandered back inside, poured coffee, and sat at the counter. The back door was still open. *Not getting up to close it.*

I checked my phone again. Nothing. I retrieved the broom and swept the kitchen. On auto-pilot, I leaned the broom against a cupboard to empty the dustpan and then put the dustpan back in the laundry room.

There was a rap at the back door, and it swung open. Alex walked in. "Sorry to bother you but your back door was ajar, and I was worried with everything that's been going on around here."

I grit my teeth. "I'm fine. I'm a little tired this morning and didn't notice it until I sat down."

"Shall I shut it?"

"No. Leave it partway open, that way the cats can come in when they want."

She studied me. "You look done in."

"There's a lot going on." I stared at the counter, hoping she would leave.

"I have just the thing. Green juice. It's so good for you. Kale, lemon, garlic, ginger, and apples, among other healthy things. You'll love it. I'll be right back." She turned and walked out the door.

Sounded disgusting. I tried to edge the door shut with my foot. My leg wasn't long enough. I sighed and put my forehead on the cool counter.

A few minutes later, Alex bustled back in. "Luckily I already had some made up from this morning." She handed me a mason jar filled to the brim with what looked like green algae.

My stomach churned. "Thanks. I'll drink it a little later." I took it from her and started for the refrigerator.

"You'll feel better if you drink it now. A good shot of veggies in the morning makes everything right."

I suppressed a groan. "I do appreciate it, but I'm waiting for a phone call, so if you don't mind." I shoved the juice in the refrigerator and turned back to Alex.

She was holding a small revolver. "I don't want to use this; I want time to establish my alibi. Get the juice, Merry."

My eyes widened. "What's in the juice?"

"I told you. Lots of great veggies. Don't worry. Everything in that glass is all-natural." She gestured with the gun. "Take it out."

I retrieved the mason jar, holding it as far away from my body as possible. "Are there castor bean hulls in here?"

"They pulverize so nicely in a coffee grinder." She barked a laugh. "Course you have to make sure you don't use it for coffee beans. That would be a nasty surprise. And you have to wear protective gear. But all in all, it's not that hard."

I gulped, "But why me?"

"I knew you wouldn't stop. I saw you. Every time you walked by my house you looked at it and frowned. I could feel your wheels turning."

"I was worried about you!"

My phone dinged with a text. I grabbed for it.

Alex swept it off the counter, and it hit the floor. "I guess you'll find out how good your protective case was. Or not. Drink the juice."

"But the muffin? Who made the muffins with peanuts in them?'

She sighed. "You're so slow. I did. I waited until I was sure Ed saw me, and then I collapsed. As he ran over, I nibbled the tiniest bit of the muffin. It was enough to send me into shock. I had my EpiPen hidden under a rock, but I didn't need to use it because Ed got help so quickly."

The phone buzzed again, and then it rang.

"Someone really wants to get in touch with you. Enough stalling, drink the juice." The revolver was pointed straight at my chest.

My hand reached for the glass as Patty barged through the back door, knocking Alex off balance. I grabbed the broom and hit Alex's hand; the gun went skidding across the floor. Alex dove for it and I landed on top of her. We scrabbled for the weapon. Alex came up with it, and Patty slammed her foot down on top of Alex's hand. The revolver discharged into my phone sending it spinning, inches from my head.

Patty stomped her foot again, and this time Alex screamed and released the gun. "You broke my hand!"

I got to my feet, kicked the gun across the room, and then ran to the laundry. I returned with two small bungee cords. I wrapped one around Alex's ankles, and Patty took the other and bound Alex's arms. Hands shaking, I picked up the gun and deposited it on the counter next to the juice.

Alex moaned.

Patty was ashen. "What on earth happened?"

I pointed toward Alex. "She killed Richard, poisoned herself to throw me off the track, and tried to kill me with that juice over there."

"This looks awful." Patty picked up the juice, studying it.

"It's called green juice. But with something special added. Ground castor bean hulls."

She set the glass down carefully.

I called the police. Alex was still moaning, so we pulled her into a sitting position. She glared at Patty. "I can't believe you broke my hand."

"Well you were going to kill my friend, so I guess we're even."

I sat on one of the kitchen chairs. "Why did you kill Richard?"

"I found out on Facebook that he and Wanda were coming to visit Rob. It was serendipity that the house next to you was available. I bought the house and settled in. Then when he got here, I followed him. I found out he liked to visit the local pastry shop early in the morning."

"So when you ran into him that day it was on purpose."

"Of course. When he turned to get the sugar for his coffee, I dumped the packet of ricin into it. He almost caught me, so I goaded him by saying that I had always planned on leaving him. He exploded. He ripped open the sugar, stirred it, and the ricin dissolved. It doesn't take effect right away. It was a bonus for me that it happened when Wanda was with him. When she was charged, it was like a two for one."

"What about Frank and Bud?"

"They were almost as bad as you. They had the nerve to show up at my house and threaten me. I waited until that evening and told them I'd meet them in their room" She tsked. "I would have preferred to use the ricin, but their size dictated the gun."

Jay and two policemen barged in the back door. I yelled, "Did you close the gate? I don't want the cats to get out!"

Patty giggled.

I frowned. "What's so funny?"

"You are. Someone tries to murder you, and all you can think about is the cats running off."

I started to titter. Pretty soon Patty and I were crying we were laughing so hard. Jay touched my arm. "Are you okay?"

I tried to nod and then dissolved into another gale of laughter.

Jay led Alex from the house, one of the policemen bagged the gun, and then the hazmat team arrived. They corralled the cats into the garage and set up a tent in the backyard. Patty and I were decontaminated, and then they went to work on my kitchen. My phone left in a bag. It was a goner.

I eyed Patty. "At least my kitchen will be spotless."

They finished their work and moved to Alex's house. Patty and I looked like refugees from a hazardous spill in the white paper gear with which they clothed us. I rescued the cats and filled their new bowls with food and water.

Patty leaned against the counter.

I hugged her. "Thanks for coming this morning. I don't think I would have survived without you."

She snapped to attention. "Oh, my goodness. With all that happened, I forgot. Come with me. Did you record the news this morning?"

"Of course. You know I like to watch the weather."

We sank onto the sofa, and she turned on the TV. She fast-forwarded and then stopped. "This is it."

The TV blared: "Breaking news. In a joint FBI and Interpol raid in London this morning, American swindler Drew March, international fashion model Arianna Flores, and an unnamed accomplice were taken into custody." The picture on the screen showed Drew being led in handcuffs out of a Tudor townhouse, Arianna trailed him, and a tall third person whose head had been covered by a raincoat was last.

"Jenny," I gasped.

ABOUT THE AUTHOR

Eileen Curley Hammond is an author who retired from a successful marketing career in the insurance industry. She and her husband share the house with two cats that are determined to train them.

For those of you who have been keeping up on this page, you know that Eileen and her husband were going to restock the fish pond this year. Happily, they now have two new koi, two shubunkins, and a school of minnows. They've also enhanced their heron defense system.

The author looks forward to continuing to write and getting some rest after a long slog gardening in the spring and summer.

www.ingramcontent.com/pod-product-compliance
Lightning Source LLC
Chambersburg PA
CBHW022137240626
47153CB00007B/2400